"You can' on love."

Panic-stricken, Carrie half twisted away from Roger.

Abruptly he straightened, the warmth draining from his face as he looked at her with contempt. "You'd trade in what we could have for a regular pay packet and a suburban bungalow? I can't believe you mean it."

Tears of frustration gathered behind her eyelids. "Is that so wrong? I saw what my mother went through for love, what she's still going through. Even now, she may have to sell her home."

Compassion warred with frustration in his face. "Maybe I could help. Just give me a chance."

How could he help? Living in borrowed homes and hotel rooms, from commission to commission. "It's no use," she said flatly. "It wouldn't work."

Valerie Parv had a busy and successful career as a journalist and advertising copywriter before she began writing for Harlequin in 1982. She is an enthusiastic member of several Australian writers' organizations. Her many interests include her husband, her cat and the Australian environment. Her love of the land is a distinguishing feature in many of her books for Harlequin. She has recently written a colorful study in a nonfiction book titled *The Changing Face of Australia*. Her home is in New South Wales.

Books by Valerie Parv

The Love Artist

Valerie Parv

Harlequin Books

TORONTO • NEW YORK • LONDON
AMSTERDAM • PARIS • SYDNEY • HAMBURG
STOCKHOLM • ATHENS • TOKYO • MILAN

Original hardcover edition published in 1986
by Mills & Boon Limited

ISBN 0-373-02860-1

Harlequin Romance first edition September 1987

CHAPTER ONE

A DEPARTMENT store was like a theatre, Carrie Doyle observed as she made her way between the counters, which were shrouded with dust covers—opening time still being an hour away. The store's customers were the audience, she decided. They were ministered to by the backstage people like the cleaners and the board. And they were looked after by what you might call the front-of-house people like the sales assistants, floor managers, and department heads such as herself.

Not quite, she reminded herself, although at twenty-six she was quite proud of being an assistant department head, especially when the department concerned one of her great enthusiasms—books.

With a feeling of satisfaction, she reached the book section office to find her boss, Helen Johanssen, unlocking the safe in which the most valuable stock was stored. From it, Helen extracted a leatherbound replica of Captain Cook's log book, faithfully executed and for sale to a collector for several hundred dollars.

'Bet we don't have that in stock for very long,' Carrie observed, stowing her handbag and jacket.

Helen frowned. 'I don't know. I still think it should have come out a little closer to the Bicentennial. Historic anniversaries always increase demand for this sort of book.'

Lovingly, she set the volume out in its display case which was wired for security, locked the case and straightened. 'Do you think you could manage the whole show on your own today?'

Since it was unusual for Helen to leave the department on a Thursday or Friday, their busiest days, Carrie tilted an eyebrow. 'Of course. What's up?'

'The fire at Rush's.' Helen named one of their main suppliers. 'A lot of their stock was water-damaged and our buyer is negotiating with them to buy it at a special price. But she wants me to assess the extent of the damage before we commit ourselves.'

'I understand. You go ahead; I'm sure I can cope. The two casuals are coming in for the lunch-hour rush in any case.'

Helen bit her lip. 'I know, and normally the three of you would breeze through, but I'm expecting Roger Torkan to drop by today to arrange a signing session for his new book.'

'What time is he due in here?'

'That's just it. He didn't say and I can't reach him to change the appointment. He's been in New Guinea for the last couple of weeks, canoeing down the Fly River or some such.'

Carrie grinned. 'Why on earth would a cartoonist be canoeing down the Fly River?'

'Search me. Maybe he enjoys roughing it in his spare time. I don't know the first thing about the man except that he's published a new collection of cartoons and I've arranged with his agent for him to sign some copies here. It should be a great sales boost.'

'Pity we don't know more about him, though. I'll bet you've heard from the publicity people about that!'

Helen grimaced. 'Have I ever? They wanted to send out press releases about his visit and there wasn't a thing I could tell them, except the brief blurb on the dust jacket of the book. Apparently he keeps his private life very separate from his professional life.'

'Don't worry about a thing,' said Carrie firmly,

sensing Helen's temptation to stay and handle the artist's visit herself. 'If he comes before you get back I'll just keep him occupied till you get here.'

'Well, if you're sure . . .'

'Of course I'm sure!'

'In that case, I'll go now. Hopefully I'll be back before he gets here. If he's like most artists, he won't wake up much before lunchtime, so I'll have time to get across town, look at the books, and be back here before he arrives.'

She ducked into her office and picked up her handbag and coat, shrugging it on as she emerged. 'There's a copy of his book on my desk. If you get a chance, have a look through it. You might pick up some clues as to how to handle him.'

She was still throwing titbits of advice over her shoulder as she left. When she'd gone, Carrie sighed with relief. Helen was a firm but pleasant boss, her one failing being a reluctance to delegate authority. She tried to do everything herself, leaving few opportunities for Carrie to demonstrate her capabilities.

Being left to run the department on one of their busy days was a real bonus. She would have to hold the fort alone until the casuals came in at eleven; then she might be able to catch up on some paperwork until the lunch-time rush began.

'On your own?' queried a cheerful voice as she headed back to the office. A tall, lanky young man sauntered over to her from the adjacent computer department and looked around. 'Don't tell me the dragon lady actually entrusted you with her precious department?'

'She isn't a dragon lady, Michael. She's just . . . efficient,' said Carrie with difficulty, feeling guilty at having been caught thinking much the same thing, except that she wouldn't dream of voicing her feelings.

'Efficient and hard,' he added, leaning against a cardboard display of a new paperback. 'Do you know she fired Rosalind yesterday?'

Carrie's head came up. Rosalind was the junior sales assistant shared by both their departments. She was also a special friend of Michael's. 'No, I didn't. Helen went out before we had time to talk. Knowing Helen, she must have had a good reason,' she added loyally.

'All right, what if Rosalind was caught out in a lie?' he said, his tone unforgiving. 'She took a "sickie" the day before and Helen met her in a restaurant downtown.'

'Then she shouldn't have lied about being ill when she really wanted some time off. You know what Helen's like about honesty. Couldn't Rosalind have taken a day's holiday if the time off was so important?'

'She'd used up all her available leave. Anyway, I can see I'll get no sympathy out of you—you're starting to sound just like Helen.'

With that, he sauntered back to his own department and began flicking dust off the racks of computer games, not looking at Carrie again.

Was she becoming like Helen? she wondered uncomfortably. She would hate to think she was as inflexible as her boss. Granted she did want to get ahead in her job—maybe even manage a bookshop herself one day. But not at the cost of turning into a martinet as, she was forced to admit, Helen sometimes appeared.

Poor Rosalind! Carrie liked the bubbly youngster, even if she was a bit irresponsible. She had brought a breath of fresh air into the department that compensated for the times when she hadn't pulled her weight. With an effort, Carrie dismissed such thoughts from her mind. There was work to be done, and without a junior she would definitely have to do everything herself until the casuals arrived.

With so much to do and customers to look after, it was coffee-break time before Carrie remembered the book Helen had left for her to read.

She collected her coffee from the canteen and took it back to the office so she would be on hand if the casuals needed her. After assuring herself that they could cope, she sat down at Helen's desk and reached for the book but was forestalled by a cheerful male voice.

'Mind if I join you?'

She looked up. 'Hello, Michael. Actually I was going to work through my coffee-break.'

'Then it's just as well I rescued you. You mustn't make yourself a slave to Petrie's, you know.'

Resignedly, she set the book aside. It would have to wait until Michael finished his break, since she knew from past experience that the only way to get rid of him was to throw him out bodily and, despite his irritating manner, she liked the young man. 'How's the computer business?' she asked.

He shrugged. 'Space Invaders out, Pac Man in, and on it goes.' He leaned forward. 'I'd rather hear how you got on with that errant little sister of yours.'

Immediately, she regretted having confided in Michael the previous day, but she had been so stunned by Krys's announcement that she was dropping out of university to become a cartoonist like their father that she had been driven to talk to someone. 'Nothing's changed,' she admitted reluctantly. 'She still thinks she has all the education she needs to make it in the art world.'

Michael sipped his coffee. 'You did say she has talent?'

'I think so. She takes after our father, I suppose. She tells me that one day she'll be exhibiting in the National Gallery like him.'

'Who knows, maybe she will!'

Carrie thought of Oscar Doyle, her father, who had left the family when she was fourteen and now lived in an artists' colony on the far north coast of the state. 'I still think living on a shoestring, from commission to commission, is no life for a young, innocent girl. And it's poor thanks to Mum for all her sacrifices. She worked so hard to put Krys through university.'

Michael's eyebrow quirked upwards. 'Do I detect a note of envy in your voice?'

'Of course not,' she said a shade too defensively, unwilling to admit that he might be right. 'I accepted long ago that there wasn't enough money for me to continue my education—that's why I'm determined to make the best of opportunities here.'

'But it isn't the same as being a school-marm?'

'I wouldn't have been a school-marm,' she snapped back. 'I'd have been a darned good teacher!' Aware that her hostility had betrayed her, she took deep calming breaths. 'Thank you, Mr Freud.'

He grinned, unabashed. 'My couch is your couch, Carrie . . . for psychoanalysis, I mean. Always glad to help.'

He drained his cup and headed back to his own department, leaving Carrie looking after him thoughtfully. There was no way she could misconstrue his remark about the couch. Michael was far too young for her, but he was uncannily perceptive sometimes. Once she had confessed her regret at not completing her education—the rest he had worked out for himself, including her hostility towards her father for leaving them penniless, and the faintest feeling of jealousy towards Krys, although it wasn't her fault that Mum was on her feet financially by the time Krys was ready for university. But it was too bad that Krys didn't appreciate her good luck.

With a sigh, she reached for the book of cartoons. Unlike Krys, Carrie was not fond of them. They reminded her painfully of her father's desertion. So she was surprised to find herself chuckling over the drawings in Roger Torkan's book. They depicted the antics of a lovable cat called Marmalade. At the same time, Carrie realised the artist was subtly satirising his fellow human beings.

'Clever,' she mused, and turned to the cover notes on the artist. But before she could read the brief biography her eyes were arrested by a large head-and-shoulders portrait of Roger Torkan.

What she had expected, she didn't know, but it certainly wasn't the forceful-looking man who stared arrogantly out at her from the dust jacket. If the colour reproduction was to be trusted, his eyes were even bluer than Paul Newman's, under heavy, brooding eyebrows. The nose was slightly snubbed, softening the impression somewhat, and he had a devastating male-model smile.

'Gay, most likely,' she said aloud, finding it easier to think that as the best line of defence against such a disturbing-looking man.

'Not even close,' said a voice from the doorway and she looked up straight into eyes that *were* bluer than Paul Newman's, although at present they had retreated into narrow slits of annoyance.

Training came quickly to her rescue and she slid smoothly from behind the desk, extending a hand to him. 'You must be Mr Torkan,' she said, flashing him her most winning smile.

It was wasted on him. 'What made you decide I must be gay, Miss . . .?'

'Ms,' she corrected automatically. 'Caroline Doyle. I'm the assistant department head.'

His gaze raked her from head to toe, until she could feel her clothes peeling away like the layers of an onion. 'Could have fooled me,' he growled. 'You look young enough to be the office junior. And you still haven't answered my question.'

This wasn't going at all the way it was supposed to, she thought frantically. She was in turn glad that Helen wasn't here to see her discomfiture and wishing that she would appear and rescue her assistant. She decided to bluff her way through. 'Look, I don't know what you thought you heard, but I was admiring the dust jacket . . . saying to myself that it's a lovely shade or *grey*.'

'Hmmm.' This time, his look held a grudging respect as he came into the office uninvited and threw himself into the visitor's chair.

'Do come in,' she said belatedly. 'Would you like some coffee?'

'Not if it means you have to go and get it.'

All the same, from the hungry way he was eyeing her cup she guessed he would appreciate some. 'It's all right. I'll have one of the casuals fetch it.'

As she retreated to the safety of the shop floor, she was relieved to find that Diane was free for the moment and didn't mind going up to the canteen to fetch another cup of coffee.

She braced herself before returning to the office. Mr Roger Torkan was going to be a handful, no doubt about it, and she hadn't helped matters by casting aspersions on his manhood before they'd even met!

'Your coffee is on its way,' she explained as she slid

back behind the desk, glad to have its reassuring bulk between them.

'Thanks. I take it Helen Johanssen is otherwise engaged?'

'Yes. She'll be back later, hopefully before you have to leave.'

He eased his shoulders back against the leather of the chair. 'No problem. I'm in no hurry. Couldn't sleep anyway so I decided to come in and get this over with.'

So Helen had been right—he was as indolent as the other artists Helen knew. 'I thought you'd be keen to meet your public,' she said, keeping the disapproval out of her tone only with an effort.

'I draw pictures for my public. They can have all of those they want. I do not see the need to make them a present of the rest of me as well.'

Uneasily, she shuffled papers around on the desk. 'In that case, I'm surprised you agreed to do the signing session.'

'I didn't, my agent did. He knows perfectly well how I feel about publicity but he took advantage of my absence to make the commitment for me, knowing also that I never renege on a commitment. I'll get the bastard for this, never you fear!'

If she had expected him to apologise for using such language in front of her, she was mistaken. He noted her look of annoyance. 'Don't care for plain speaking, do you? I never knew a woman who did. You all prefer empty flattery to a few home truths.'

'Let's just say that I've found a little civility doesn't hurt in business,' she said mildly, unwilling to be drawn into a discussion of her personality. Until now, she had avoided looking too directly at him, but now she faced him defiantly, almost gasping at the raw power she saw in those dazzling blue eyes. They were so magnetic that they tended to blind one to his dishevelled appearance. Scruffy might actually be a better word.

Granted, his physique was imposing. When he stood in the doorway he nudged the top lintel, so he must be over six feet tall, and there was an air of strength in those massively male shoulders and powerful, assured movements. But his clothes were faded and—yes— dirty, as if he had slept a night or two in them. A two-day growth of straw-coloured beard stubbled his chin, adding to his air of menace.

'Not what you expected a famous artist to look like, huh?' he commented, apparently reading her mind.

'Cartoonist,' she corrected unthinkingly.

At once, his frown deepened. 'Artist, ' he repeated with a touch of savagery. 'You say cartoonist as if it's a dirty word.'

This was hopeless. She spread her hands palm-upwards, unaware of how appealingly vulnerable the gesture made her look. 'I'm sorry, I didn't mean that the way it sounded. As a matter of fact, I enjoyed reading your book just now. It's just that . . . well, cartoonists aren't my favourite people, that's all. No fault of yours, and nothing you can do to change it, I'm afraid.'

'I wouldn't be too sure of that. Let me guess. You had a lover who was a cartoonist and he "done you wrong".'

Laughing in spite of herself, she shook her head. 'It was my father, actually, and it's too long a story to go into now.'

There was a definite light of interest in his eyes now, almost obliterating the traces of redness which flecked them. 'Then tell me when we can go into it.'

She stared at him. Good grief, a moment ago he had been tearing her to shreds and now he was making a pass at her. 'I'll let you know if the opportunity comes up,' she assured him, congratulating herself on fielding the implied invitation successfully without offending him.

'I believe in making my opportunities,' he said, puncturing her cool again. 'Why don't you have dinner with me tonight?'

Had he looked a little less dissipated, she might have been tempted to say yes. But she was instinctively wary of his too-masculine appeal, forcing herself to see what his personality was trying to make her overlook. The magnetic blue eyes were bloodshot, from too much good living, no doubt. And the designer jeans and T-shirt he wore had defintely seen better days.

She would be a fool to encourage him. Hadn't she learned anything from her father? 'Thanks for the invitation, but no, thank you,' she said, trying to inject a note of finality into her voice. 'Ah, here's your coffee.'

'Saved by the bell,' he said grudgingly, then sighed. 'I suppose you're going to insist on talking about the bloody ... pardon me ... the book signing.'

They'd achieved that much at least, she told herself, trying to repress a twinge of regret at turning down his invitation.

She waited until Diane had placed his coffee before him and returned to the department before turning the discussion to the details of the signing session. He listened dutifully as she outlined Helen's plans and pointed out the location in the deparment where the dais was to be set up.

'Do I have to be on a pedestal?' he groaned.

'I'd have thought you were used to it,' she rejoined.

'Oh, you would, would you? You have me neatly pigeon-holed under D for dislike. Which is hardly fair considering we've only just met.' He leaned forward, resting his chin on one hand. 'Tell me, are you always so quick to pass judgments, *Ms* Doyle?'

Only for certain men in certain occupations, she thought fleetingly, but resisted the temptation to say so. She didn't owe him any explanations. 'I haven't passed judgment, as you put it,' she rejoined coldly. 'If you come in here looking like a . . . a derelict, you shouldn't be surprised if women don't fly into your arms.'

His eyebrows arched ironically. 'Would a pinstriped suit and tie create a better impression with you?'

Since he didn't look as if he owned either garment she was safe in admitting, 'They might.'

Instantly, his eyes retreated into their angry slits and his mouth twisted into a sneer. 'Well, that's just too damned bad, isn't it? You really take the cake, you women's lib types. You reserve the right to be whatever you want to be, but heaven help any man who claims the same privilege!'

It was presumptuous of him to attack her like this, especially when he couldn't know what had made her so conservative. 'Now who's making judgments?' she demanded. 'You don't know the first thing about me, yet you barge in here and verbally attack me just because I refuse to have dinner with you. Of all the overbearing, egotistical . . .'

She tailed off as she saw the colour drain from his face and he leaned back in the chair, closing his eyes. 'I'm sorry,' he said hoarsely. 'I should have known better than to come in here now. When I couldn't get to sleep, it seemed like a good idea, but I can see now it was my mistake.'

To her dismay, he stood up and stretched as if to ease painfully cramped muscles. 'Where are you going?' she said. 'We . . . we haven't finished.'

'We never even got started, as you so properly reminded me,' he replied dully. 'Pretend I haven't been here this morning. I'll be at my hotel if Helen

Johanssen wants to get in touch with me.'

Now she'd done it! By letting him bait her with his chauvinistic remarks, she had made a complete mess of a simple task. She could imagine what Helen would say when she returned to find that none of the arrangements for the signing had been finalised. 'That's right, walk out on me like a coward,' she snapped, barely aware of having spoken aloud.

His head swivelled around and his eyes flashed warning fire. 'What did you call me?'

Despair made her reckless. 'You come in here with your chauvinistic attitudes and expect me to swoon at the prospect of going out with you. Then because I demur, you walk out, knowing I'll get hell from my boss.'

He braced himself against the door frame. 'I can't win with you, can I? I'm an overbearing, egotistical chauvinist if I stay . . . and a coward if I go. Would you mind telling me what *would* make you happy?'

Abashed because she could see his point, she looked down at her fingers, noting idly that the polish was chipped on one nail. She curled the offending finger into her palm and took a deep breath. 'It would make me happy if you sat down again and we finished making arrangements,' she said meekly. 'I'm sorry if I seem hard to please, it's just . . .'

His expression was unforgiving. 'Cartoonists aren't your favourite people. I know, you told me.'

All the same, the light of battle faded from his eyes and he turned back into the office. Suddenly, he began to sway and gripped the edge of the desk for support.

Instantly, Carrie was on her feet and moving around to his side of the desk. 'What's the matter? Are you ill?'

He shook his head as if to clear it. 'This is what comes of having no sleep for three days. Then when you try to rest, you're beyond sleeping.'

Their differences forgotten, she slid an arm around his waist, feeling the hardness of his body beneath the thin T-shirt. 'You'd better sit down before you fall down.'

He leaned heavily against her, taking slow, deep breaths. Suddenly he realised the position they were in. 'Aren't you afraid I'll take advantage of this?' he asked, indicating her embracing arm.

'In what way?' she asked, still distracted by concern for him.

'By doing this.'

Before she could anticipate his action, he brought his lips hard against hers. The contact held fire and passion and she drew a sharp breath, her eyes startled. But it wasn't the shock of being kissed by him which startled her. Rather, it was the reciprocal stirring she felt in her own body. She knew she should pull away but instead, she found herself kissing him back with matching fervour. The door swung open and Helen came in, breathless and red-cheeked from hurrying. Confronted by the sight of her assistant and Roger Torkan locked in each other's arms, she froze. 'Well!'

Like a guilty schoolchild, Carrie sprang away from Roger but he merely straightened and held out his hand. 'You must be Mrs Johanssen,' he said easily.

Still nonplussed, Helen shook his hand limply. 'I didn't know that you two knew each other,' she said a little faintly.

'We didn't. We were just rectifying that,' responded Roger.

He was unperturbed by the situation, although Carrie's cheeks burned with embarrassment. He didn't know Helen as well as her assistant did. She wouldn't say anything while Roger was still here but as soon as he left, Carrie would have some explaining to do. What she was going to say in her defence, she didn't know. Never before had she behaved so badly. Helen had a right to be scandalised—Carrie was equally appalled by her own behaviour.

She sat in mortified silence while Helen plunged into a discussion with Roger, although now and then her gaze flickered questioningly across to Carrie. Roger must have recoverd from his spell of weakness, although not completely or Carrie was sure he wouldn't have been so compliant, he nodded agreement with Helen over each point, not even demurring when Helen confirmed that he would appear on a raised dais in the centre of the department.

Inevitably, the meeting ended and Roger rose to leave, uncoiling his considerable length from the chair with the grace of a panther, albeit a weary-looking one. He moved towards the door then paused, turning back to hand a card to Carrie. Without looking at it, she dropped it into her handbag, wanting only for him to leave so she could make peace with Helen.

Her boss's tight-lipped expession made it clear that it wasn't going to be easy. 'Would you mind telling me what that was all about?' she asked coldly as soon as the door closed behind Roger.

'We were discussing the book-signing session as you requested . . .' Carrie began awkwardly.

'It looked like it!' Helen snorted. 'How long had that discussion been going on?'

'Nothing happened until the few minutes before you came back. He looked as if he was going to pass out with exhaustion and I propped him up. That's when he . . . kissed me.'

At once, Helen's frown vanished. 'So it wasn't your

fault after all. He was the one taking advantage of the situation.'

Miserably, Carrie looked away. It would be so easy to say it was Roger's fault, but she couldn't let him take all the blame when she was a willing accomplice. 'That's not really fair, either,' she said softly. 'I didn't exactly try to resist him.'

'Well, I can't damn you for your honesty,' Helen said unwillingly. She braced herself on the edge of her desk. 'Can't you see, Carrie, when you behave like that you set the cause of women in business back ten years? Would he have behaved like that if you'd been a man?'

'No, of course not.'

'Then why should it be acceptable because you're a woman? Next time, try and keep things a bit more businesslike, will you?'

Carrie nodded contritely, glad that the worst seemed to be over. 'It won't happen again,' she assured her boss.

'Very well, we'll say no more about it then.' Helen glanced at her watch. 'You'd better go to early lunch.'

Thankful for the reprieve, Carried snatched up her handbag and hurried out of the department. Only when she reached the sanctuary of the canteen and settled down with coffee and her home-made chicken sandwiches, did she remember the card Roger had handed her.

It was his business card, containing a Central Coast telephone number and an appealing caricature of himself. Handwritten on the back was the name of a hotel along with a telephone and room number—his Sydney address, she assumed.

Was this an invitation to her to contact him? If so, she certainly wasn't going to do any such thing. She'd been lucky in getting off so lightly after the disgraceful scene Helen had interrupted this morning—she wasn't going to risk a repetition.

She had never behaved like that in her life. She didn't even have the excuse of being a complete innocent, having never been short of dates, so she should have known better than to leave herself open like that.

She must be out of her mind! She didn't even like Roger very much. He was unkempt and dissipated-looking, freely admitting that he hadn't slept in three days. He looked as if he'd spent most of them in a bar somewhere.

Yet Carrie couldn't deny that he had affected her strongly. In a ridiculously short space of time, he had aroused in her a whole range of sensations that hungered for release.

What was worse, he had known exactly what effect he was having on her, being sure enough of her attraction to him to know that if he did kiss her, she wouldn't cry 'sexual harassment'. How could she, when they both knew she had enjoyed his kiss as much as he did?

Giving herself a shake of impatience, she went back to work, determined to immerse hereself in her job to crowd out all thoughts of this morning. By mid-afternoon, she had almost managed to convince herself she had imagined the whole episode. The illusion would have been complete if not for the way her pulses raced so violently whenever she thought about the warmth of his lips on hers.

If her customers found her even more attentive than usual, they appreciated it without understanding the reason. She even earned a commendation from Helen when she interested one of their best customers, Bianca West, in the Captain Cook log book, which, she said, would make a perfect birthday present for her brother.

As Carrie did the paperwork, Helen patted her on the shoulder. 'Good work,' she mouthed, gesturing towards the customer who waited with barely concealed impatience.

Carrie gave the woman the forms to sign. 'There you are, Miss West. We have a special protective case for the book so I'll be a few more minutes packing it for you.'

Bianca sniffed tautly. 'Don't hurry on my account, will you!'

Ignoring the taunt, Carrie smiled brightly. 'Have you heard that Roger Torkan is coming here next week to sign his new book? I can set a copy aside for you, if you like.'

Bianca followed Carrie's glance towards the large poster of Roger that Helen had just finished hanging on the wall of the department. 'Not bad,' she observed. 'Is he really as dishy as that, or did they retouch the photo?'

Remembering the unkempt individual who had kissed her only hours ago, Carrie wondered how to answer. She settled for, 'Why don't you come and meet him, and find out for yourself?'

'I might just do that,' Bianca said with a note of interest in her voice. Absently, she accepted her parcel from Carrie and left without a backward glance.

'That one sale will ensure we make budget this week,' Helen said, beaming. Now that Carrie had redeemed herself, she seemed willing to forget the morning's incident.

If only Carrie could dismiss it so easily.

CHAPTER TWO

FOR the first time in two days, Carrie found herself thinking about something other than her sister's future as she rode the crowded commuter train home.

Try as she might to blot it out, Roger's image stayed in her mind, so that she read the same lines of the evening paper over and over without comprehending them. At last she folded the paper. Damn Roger Torkan! In the space of a few minutes, he had made a devastating impact on her mind and body. For it was not only her thoughts he haunted—the heady memory of his kiss lingered on her lips as well.

She wondered what Krys would think of the incident—not that Carrie intended to tell her. Even though Krys was nineteen, Carrie still considered herself responsible for her sister. This role was encouraged by their mother, Kay, who had her hands full running a guesthouse in the Blue Mountains. Living so far from Sydney, Kay was grateful that Carrie was so responsible, saving her worrying about her high-spirited younger daughter.

Responsible! The thought made Carrie grimace. What would Mum say if she knew how her 'responsible' daughter had behaved today? Wasn't Carrie supposed to be the reliable one—the one who took after her mother instead of her irresponsible father? She bit her knuckles in apprehension. What if today was a sign that she possessed more of her father's traits than she allowed for?

She shook her head, banishing the thought. Today

was an aberration. It didn't mean anything—not if she was determined not to let it.

'What are you looking so grim about?' Krys asked when she saw Carrie's set expression as she let herself into their shared flat. 'If you've come home ready to start on me again, I may as well tell you you're wasting your time. My mind is made up.'

'I know and I wasn't thinking about you,' Carrie said, startling her sister. 'I had . . . other things on my mind.' If Krys only knew!

Her sister looked curious but said nothing, clasping floury hands together. 'I've put dinner on—will savoury pancakes be all right?'

Distracted, Carrie nodded. 'Yes, fine.' Since Krys was still hovering nearby she said, 'Was there something else?'

'I had a call from Mum this afternoon. She said to give you her love.'

'How did she take your news?'

Krys bit her lip. 'I didn't tell her. I said I was coming up to the mountains this weekend, so I'll tell her then.'

'It would be better than a telephone call,' Carrie agreed, feeling a sudden surge of hope. The weekend was still a full day away. Maybe by then she could persuade Krys to change her mind, avoiding the need for the trip altogether.

'I know what you're thinking,' Krys said, surprising her. 'You hope that by Saturday I'll have come to my senses. Well, I can promise you I won't. I've thought about this long and hard and I'm convinced it's the right thing for me to do.' She patted her sister's hand, heedless of the flour which drifted on to Carrie's sleeve. 'It's OK, sis, I've already made some enquiries. I should be able to sell some of my line drawings. I do have a few contacts in the art world, you know.'

A sudden thought made Carrie smile but she masked it quickly, not wanting to alert Krys. So do I, she thought smugly. *So do I*!

If anyone could convince Krys of the folly of her action, it was Roger Torkan. He wouldn't even have to say anything. His example would be enough to show Krys what she was giving up by quitting school.

As soon as she saw what a scruffy, dissipated individual Roger was, she would be repelled by the prospect of becoming like him. Carrie knew her sister; she enjoyed wearing the latest fashions, going to newly released films and eating in good restaurants. Once she saw that her chosen career would put all this beyond her reach, she was bound to have second thoughts.

'What scheme are you hatching?' Krys asked suspiciously.

Carrie schooled her features into a mask of innocence. 'Why do I have to be scheming? I just had a good idea, that's all. Tell me—will those pancakes of yours freeze for later?'

'They should do. Why?'

'Well, we've been invited out to dinner tonight by someone I met through work. I wasn't going to accept but after your news tonight, I think you'd benefit from meeting him. He's a professional artist.'

Krys's eyes sparkled with interest, then she looked uncertain. 'Are you sure this isn't a scheme to get me to change my mind?'

Carrie shot her a look of appeal. 'Would I do a thing like that?'

'Yes, you would.'

'Of course, if you'd rather not come.'

Curiosity triumphed over suspicion and Krys let out a sharp breath of exasperation. 'You know I'm dying to meet him—as long as you're sure it's business and not a date he wants. I don't fancy playing gooseberry all evening.'

Carrie rolled her eyes expressively. 'For heaven's sake, I only met him for the first time today! You can't possibly develop a romance in such a short time.'

Can't you? she asked herself as Krys went into the bedroom to get ready. Until this morning, she would have laughed at the idea of becoming romantically involved with a man in such a short time. Now, she wasn't so sure. She remembered all too clearly the feel of his lean body aligned with hers, and the warmth of his mouth as he tasted her kiss.

A pang of guilt pierced her at the way she planned to use him this evening. Granted, he had tricked her into kissing him, getting her into trouble with Helen, but that didn't give her the right to take advantage of him in return. If he had forced himself on her, it might have been justified but she knew only too well that she had no such excuse.

Krys's future was at stake, Carrie reminded herself as she took his card out of her handbag and went to the telephone. It wasn't that she wanted to see him again herself, she thought resolutely, dialling the number. She was only doing this to help Krys.

Her heart thudded uncomfortably as she waited for the hotel to answer, then for the operator to put her through to Roger's room. He picked up the phone on the second ring. At least she hadn't interrupted his sleep.

'Torkan here,' he said crisply.

She started. Was this the same bleary-eyed creature who had weaved out of Helen's office this morning? 'It's Caroline Doyle, from Petrie's book department,' she said, aware of how her voice trembled with nervousness.

'Ah, the delectable Ms Doyle,' he said, a trace of amusement in his tone. 'I suppose you're calling to tick me off about my forward behaviour this morning?'

'Actually, I hadn't given it a thought,' she lied.

'Then your rather formidable boss didn't chew you up for improper behaviour with a client?'

She hesitated, and he sensed her unspoken reply. 'I see, she didn't care for such goings on in her office. Shall I call her and tell her it was all my fault?'

Alarmed, she answered a shade too quickly. 'No, don't do that. Besides, you . . . you weren't entirely to blame. I could have stopped you if I'd wanted to.'

'Then I was right in assuming you didn't want to?'

'Yes . . . no! I mean . . . I did get a bit carried away. Normally, I'm a lot more . . . restrained. I don't know what possessed me this morning.'

'Well I do,' he chuckled. 'It's called sexual attraction. The old "across a crowded room" stuff. And now you're calling to tell me you simply have to see me again?'

She bridled at his presumptuousness. If she didn't need his help to dissuade Krys from her chosen career, he would be the last person she'd think of calling. 'I think you're reading too much into a simple kiss,' she said, as coolly as she could. 'In fact, I'm calling to find out if your dinner invitation still stands or if you've made other plans by now.'

'Nothing I can't cancel,' he said, unperturbed by her formality. He must be very sure he could break down her reserve any time he chose, to be so heedless of her displeasure. 'The only question is—how come you want to see me again if I'm reading too much into a simple kiss?'

'I . . . I'll explain when I see you,' she evaded. If she told him the real reason for the meeting, he would never come—and she simply *had* to make Krys realise the folly of her course before she upset Kay with her news.

'Ah, a mystery woman,' he breathed. 'Don't tell me—we'll meet under a clock tower and you'll be wearing a red carnation in your lapel.'

'Nothing of the sort,' she snapped, well aware that he had completely misconstrued her call. In spite of her denials, he thought she wanted to see him again for his own sake. Well, it wouldn't hurt him to be taken down a peg. Serve him right for thinking he knew so much about her! She smiled as she imagined his surprise when he found out that they were dining with her teenage sister—not romantically *à deux* as he evidently believed.

'Very well, just tell me the time and place and I'll be there,' he said with mock resignation.

An imp of mischief made her say, 'How about Tosca's? It's a charming little French restaurant in a converted terrace house in Paddington—very cosy and intimate,' she added wickedly.

She didn't add that it was the place where Petrie's executives took their expense-account customers. It was outrageously expensive and pretentious. It was also the ideal place to show him up in contrast to his surroundings, creating just the effect she wanted Krys to witness.

'Sounds good,' he mused. 'I'll pick you up at your place. Seven-thirty OK?'

'Fine,' she agreed, and gave him the address. With a sigh of satisfaction, she replaced the receiver. Her conscience told her she was being unscrupulous. He would be like a fish out of water in a place like Tosca's. But hadn't he earned it after this morning, getting her into trouble with her boss? If he hadn't been so arrogantly confident that any woman—herself included—should fall at his feet, she wouldn't even contemplate what she was about to do.

To give herself courage for the ordeal ahead, she dressed with even more care than usual, exchanging her two-piece linen business suit for a peach chiffon chemise that buttoned all the way down the back. Her ash-brown hair had been recently highlighted with henna, and a vigorous brushing soon shaped it into a gleaming cap which hugged her head.

Simple gold disc earrings and a strand of gold chain around her neck completed the outfit. Her complexion was flawless luckily and she took great pains to keep it as clear as glass, so she needed only a light foundation and lip gloss to bring out her skin's golden undertones. Her eyelashes were naturally dark so she brushed them for extra fullness and smudged on a honey-coloured eyeshadow, shading it to peach at the edges, then fringed her lashes with mascara and she was ready. At least, outwardly she was ready. Inwardly she was wondering just what she'd got herself into. A good thing she would have Krys there as chaperon—a role reversal if ever there was one—so Roger wouldn't be able to get up to anything! She didn't doubt that he was expecting a romantic evening. Despite her protestations, he was bound to think she wanted to continue where they had left off in the office this morning.

Which was nonsense, of course.

'Wow! Do you always look this glamorous when you go out on business?'

Carrie spun around. Krys had changed into a filmy crêpe overshirt and pyjama pants hand-painted in a multi-coloured floral design. With her blonde hair tied to one side of her head in a high ponytail, she looked older than her nineteen years.

'Look who's talking!' retorted Carrie. 'You're not exactly casual yourself.'

'You never know when a contact is going to be important,' Krys confided. 'If this guy's such a professional, he could be very useful to my career.'

Since this was the opposite of what Carrie had in mind, she looked quickly away. 'You'd better put some shoes on. He'll be here in half an hour.'

With a squeal, her sister disappeared into her own room and Carrie heard her rummaging about in her wardrobe. A series of thuds indicated she was discarding one pair of shoes after another. Finally, she came back to Carrie with a theatrical sigh of despair. 'It's no good. I haven't any shoes to go with this outfit.'

'You should have considered that before you bought it,' her sister said unhelpfully, fairly sure what was coming next.

She wasn't disappointed. 'Your raffia sandals would be perfect for it,' Krys wheedled. 'You will let me borrow them, won't you? I'll take *such* good care of them.'

'And I'm the Tsar of Russia,' added Carrie, knowing she would be lucky if the shoes were even cleaned before being returned to her—assuming they were returned at all. 'Oh, go ahead.'

'Thanks, you're an angel.'

Her sister dived for Carrie's wardrobe and found the shoes she wanted, after throwing out half a dozen pairs. They were left on the floor and Carrie picked them up resignedly. She loved Krys dearly but just now and again she wished she would develop a sense of responsibility. She prayed that when Krys saw how disreputable Roger looked, she would come to her senses. It was all very well for a man like Oscar to survive on what he could earn from his drawings. At least he was in no physical danger. For an attractive girl like Krys to try to live the same way was asking for trouble.

Surprisingly, Carrie found she didn't resent her father for deserting them. In a way, she even understood his need to be by himself and dedicate himself to his art. But she did resent Oscar leaving them so poorly provided for that she was forced to leave school early to help her mother support the family until the guesthouse began to pay its way.

It was all in the past now, as Krys had so wisely pointed out. Carrie couldn't change her wayward father, but she could try to stop Krys from making the same mistakes.

The peal of the doorbell startled her out of her reverie but she willed herself to remain in her room. Let Krys answer the door. The sooner she saw what sort of life was ahead of her, the better.

'Carrie! Roger's here!' Krys trilled a few minutes later.

So it was 'Roger' already! Carrie waited a further few minutes, listening to the murmur of voices from the living-room, until her curiosity got the better of her. With deliberate slowness, she picked up her slim black evening bag and walked out into the living-room. Although not given to swearing, she almost forgot herself and used one of her father's choicer epithets as she caught sight of Roger.

He rested elegantly against the mantelpiece, his height making the small room seem even more cramped than usual. His Venetian gaberdine suit was a classic double-breasted design that fitted him like the proverbial second skin, having been carefully chosen to suit his lean proportions. The fine contrasting thread of the pinstripe was echoed in the silk tie knotted casually at his throat and there was a matching handkerchief spilling from his breast pocket.

'Roger?' she queried uncertainly.

'You look like you're seeing a ghost,' he murmured. 'Is something wrong?'

There was and he knew it! 'You look ... different from this morning.'

His answering grin was wry. 'You made it quite clear you would prefer to see me in something more conservative, so here I am.'

Her heart sank. Here he was indeed! If only he had waited just one more day before trying so hard to please her. Where were the three-day growth of yellow beard, the bloodshot eyes and weaving walk, that were supposed to influence Krys against taking up an art career?

Just in time, Carrie realised that a rented suit and a shave were unlikely to have changed the dissipated individual underneath. He was bound to reveal his true character by the time dinner was over.

Dinner! She had almost forgotten the reason for accepting his invitation. 'There's something I have to tell you,' she ventured. 'I ... ah ... invited my sister to join us this evening. I hope you don't mind.'

Since Krys was sitting on the couch gazing up at him in blatant adoration, he could hardly be anything but gracious. 'Of course I don't mind—Krys, isn't it? Your sister introduced herself while you were getting ready,' he explained in answer to Carrie's quizzically raised eyebrow.

A cream Mercedes hire-car awaited them outside and Roger courteously handed the two girls into the spacious back seat and took the seat beside the driver. The two men began to exchange polite conversation about the weather and the state of the traffic as they joined the flow of cars heading across the Harbour Bridge to the city.

Krys nudged her sister. 'He's gorgeous!' she breathed into Carrie's ear. 'If he means anything to you, you'd better warn me now because I'm planning to fall heavily in love this evening.'

'Krys! Don't be ridiculous. He's years older than you and not at all the way he looks tonight, believe me.'

'What's wrong with the way he looks? I think he's fantastic.'

'Looks can be deceptive,' was all Carrie would say. She knew her sister. Words alone would never convince her of Roger's true nature. She would have to wait until he disgraced himself at the restaurant. Then Krys would see for herself that he wasn't the sophisticated man he appeared to be.

She held her tongue all the way to Paddington, answering Krys and Roger in monosyllables, only coming to life when they pulled up outside the lovely old sandstone terrace that had been rescued from demolition and converted into a currently fashionable restaurant.

'I hope they won't mind that there's three of us instead of two,' she said sweetly as they entered. 'I should have told you before you made the reservation but . . .'

'But you had something of your own in mind,' he said shrewdly. 'I'm sure it wasn't because you felt you needed a chaperon.'

'After this morning, I could be forgiven for thinking so,' she murmured.

He frowned but before he could reply, the manager swept towards them. 'Good evening sir, ladies,' he said as his eyes wandered appreciatively over the sisters.

Carrie braced herself. She knew this particular man—he was more of a snob than most of his customers, delighting in putting down anyone he

decided was beneath the restaurant's usual high
standard. What he would say when Roger insisted on
changing their reservation, she didn't like to think.

To her amazement, Roger said something softly into
the man's ear and they shook hands lightly, then the
man smiled greasily and nodded. He led the party
through the formal restaurant with its sandblasted
brick walls, sepia photographs, stuffed birds and
hanging lanterns, up a short flight of stairs to a
curtained alcove. In the centre was an oval table set
with starched pink napkins. There were four place
settings and the man gestured to a waitress who swiftly
removed one setting.

He half bowed to Roger. 'Will this be to your liking?'

'Perfectly, thank you,' Roger assured him.

Carrie's mouth dropped open. What on earth had
Roger said to the man to make him so attentive to their
needs? Obviously, some money had changed hands at
the reception desk, but so discreetly that she couldn't be
sure. All of which made Roger Torkan seem very much
at home in his surroundings.

She squirmed uncomfortably, suddenly sure that the
evening wasn't going to go the way she had planned
after all.

Roger noticed her discomfort. 'Is something wrong?'
he asked.

'No, this is lovely, thank you. It's just . . .'

'You expected me to make a fool of myself in such a
setting, right?'

His tone was so deceptively mild that it was a
moment before she realised what he'd just said. 'I don't
know what you're talking about,' she said, forcing a
laugh.

'Don't you? You were surprised when I turned up at
your place looking so respectable, and since you chose

the restaurant, it can only mean you expected me to look out of place here. Why, I wonder?'

She glanced quickly at Krys but her sister was absorbed in her favourite activity of people-watching, scanning the restaurant from their raised vantage point with total concentration. She hadn't heard Roger's aside to Carrie.

'That's a crazy idea,' she said shakily. 'I happen to like this place, that's all.'

'You disappoint me, then. Despite your attempts to seem stuffy and conservative, I wouldn't have thought that such a blatantly trendy set-up would appeal to you.'

'There you go again,' she bridled, 'thinking you know so much about me.'

'Not as much as I'd like to know,' he said, his tone caressing.

She had a brief respite while they placed their orders. She chose breast of duck in a light peppercorn sauce, while Roger and Krys both selected rainbow trout. Carrie had another surprise when Roger went into consultation with the wine waiter, turning out to be knowledgeable about Australian wines, finally choosing a 1981 Chablis to complement their food.

'Happy with my performance so far?' he asked Carrie, arching one eyebrow ironically.

Was all this an act to impress her? she wondered fleetingly then acknowledged that it was unlikely. The more she saw of him in these surroundings, the more it seemed that this morning was the aberration. If so, he wasn't going to be much help in getting Krys to change her mind.

'Krys was telling me she wants to be a professional cartoonist,' he said, divining her train of thought yet again.

'As of two days ago,' Carrie commented drily.

Krys gave her a withering look. 'Maybe that was when I announced my decision, but I've been planning it for a long time.'

'I see. And what is your particular area of interest?'

'Black and white line work,' Krys said promptly. 'My father says I have a talent for it.'

'I take it your father knows something about art?'

'He's an artist—Oscar Doyle. Perhaps you've heard of him?'

Poor Krys! When would she learn that very few people had heard of their father, however much Krys hero-worshipped him? To her surprise, Roger said, 'As a matter of fact, I have. I've seen some of his work in the National Gallery.'

Krys's eyes shone and the look she gave Carrie plainly said, 'I told you so.' 'Tell me what you think of his work,' she prompted, leaning forward with childish eagerness.

To Carrie's annoyance, Roger was happy to oblige, and the two of them were soon engrossed in a discussion of the finer points of black and white line work. They stopped only long enough to attend to the excellent food that was set before them, but Roger was soon back to making points with his fork-tip again.

Belatedly, Krys remembered Carrie's presence. 'I'm so glad you thought of inviting me tonight,' she exclaimed. 'Roger and I have so much in common.'

An unexpected pang shot through Carrie. When Roger began to sketch rapidly on one of the table napkins, she felt tears of frustration prickle behind her eyes and she got up quickly, glancing around for the location of the ladies' room. 'Excuse me,' she said to no one in particular, and fled.

In the cloakroom, she leaned against a hand basin and took a deep breath. She couldn't be jealous of the

way Krys and Roger were getting on so well together—
could she? Granted, she did feel left out of the
specialised conversation, but that was the only thing
troubling her, surely ...

Repairing her make-up boosted her flagging spirits a
little and she managed a bright smile to mask her
feeling of despair as she returned to the table. Roger
was alone.

'Where's Krys?' she asked, looking around.

'A very dashing young man came up and asked her to
dance and I urged her to accept,' he explained. 'I
thought it was time you got a word in edgewise.'

'I was quite happy listening to you two,' she assured
him rather too emphatically. 'I thought Krys would
enjoy meeting a professional in her favourite field,
which was why I suggested this dinner.'

His eyes bored into her like gimlets. 'Are you sure
that was the reason? Or was it because you hoped I
would put Krys off the idea of becoming a cartoonist?'

'Whatever gives you that idea?' she asked weakly.

'It's the only answer that fits. Unluckily for you, your
sister is a lot more ingenuous and told me all about her
ambitions—and your disapproval of them. It wasn't
hard to put two and two together. You thought the way
I looked at your office this morning was the way I
always looked and you were counting on that to
convince Krys that all artists are no-hopers, weren't
you?'

Defiantly, she lifted her head. 'All right, what if I
was?'

His fingers clamped over her wrist with a grip of
steel. 'Then you admit it?'

Tears of indignation sprang to her eyes and she
blinked them away. 'Yes, I admit it. Now let me go.'

'Not so fast. I don't appreciate being used, Ms Doyle,

and you've just admitted you were using me tonight. I think you owe me an apology.'

Unhappily, she dropped her head forward. 'You're right, it was a rotten thing to do and I'm sorry—truly I am.'

At once, he released her hand. 'That's better. I'd hate to think that the passionate woman I kissed this morning was a nasty little schemer.'

Colour rushed to her cheeks. 'By the same token, you can hardly blame me for thinking the man I met this morning was the real Roger Torkan. I'm still not sure which of you is real!'

'Then we'll have to do something about that, won't we?'

'What do you have in mind?'

'Another get-together—this time without the deception. I'd like a chance to explain about this morning, for one thing.'

'You don't owe me any explanations,' she said quickly.

'I think I do. You got quite the wrong idea about me today and I'd like to correct that. Will you see me again?'

Common sense told her to end this while she still could but something deeper prompted her to say, 'Yes, all right.'

'Good. Krys has asked me to look at some of her work and I've agreed, which should provide a good excuse for us to see each other again.'

At the mention of Krys's work, she balked. This was the very thing she had feared. Krys was already smitten with Roger and the more she saw of him, the more she would try to imitate his lifestyle. 'I wish you wouldn't encourage Krys in this crazy plan of hers.'

'Who says it's crazy?' He was annoyed, she could see

from the white flecks radiating out from his pupils. 'If it's what she wants to do and she's capable of it, who are you to stop her?'

'Someone who cares about her and doesn't want to see her get hurt,' she said quietly.

'All I can say is, you have a funny way of showing it,' he derided, snapping his fingers for their bill. 'I think it's time somebody showed you that you can't go through life manipulating people. You tried to do it with me tonight and now you want to do it with your sister's life.'

She tossed her head at him. 'And who's going to teach me this lesson—you?' she demanded.

His gaze travelled deliberately over her upper body, lingering on the deep cleft between her breasts, which was emphasised by the scalloped cut of her dress. 'It might be a challenge at that,' he mused.

Something threatening, and at the same time thrilling, in his tone warned her that it was a challenge she would have a hard time meeting.

CHAPTER THREE

CARRIE invited Roger to join them for dinner on Saturday night. She was unprepared for her sister's wail of dismay when she broke the news to her after Roger dropped them back at their flat.

'I told you I'll be away this weekend. I want to tell Mum about my plans before . . . before she hears it from someone else.'

Carrie reddened. 'You don't think I'd do such a rotten thing?'

'I suppose not, but I won't feel at ease about it until I've told her.'

Still hurt by the implied accusation, Carrie turned away. 'I'd better call Roger tomorrow and tell him not to come.'

Indecision flickered across Krys's attractive features as she wrestled with the desire for Roger to see her work, and the need to talk to her mother. 'Why put him off? You'll be here, won't you?'

Carrie's mouth tightened but she nodded. 'I will, but I thought it was your work he was coming to see.'

'You can show it to him. I'll leave my sketches out for you. In any case, he won't give you his opinion on the spot. He'll probably want to think about it before he gives me a verdict.' She tugged at Carrie's arm. 'Please, do me this favour? He might say my work is no good, and then I'd have to go back to university, wouldn't I?'

For a brief moment, Carrie allowed herself to hope it might work out that way before she saw through Krys's strategy. 'You'll only accept his opinion if it agrees with yours,' she said heavily. 'You know you will.'

Krys was too transparent, and had been since she was a child. Sent to her room for demanding something she couldn't have, she would emerge half an hour later, apologetic on the surface, then proceed to steer the conversation around to her original demand. Usually she got her own way. They were both grown up now but in this respect nothing had changed.

'All right,' Carrie conceded. 'I'll entertain Roger for you and show him your drawings.'

At the same time, she wondered how honest she was being with Krys. The idea of spending another evening with Roger was appealing. He was undeniably attractive and personable, despite her unfortunate first impression of him. She did want to know why he looked so terrible when he turned up at the store this morning.

Krys enveloped her in a bone-shattering hug. 'You're a doll, Carrie. I owe you one.'

Add it to the collection, Carrie thought wryly. If Krys ever started to repay all the favours she'd chalked up with Carrie, she would never stop. All the same, she smiled at her sister with genuine affection. She was still such a child, even at nineteen, and desperately striving for an air of sophistication.

Suddenly she felt twice as old as her twenty-six years. Why couldn't she be carefree and girlish like Krys, anticipating Roger's visit with enthusiasm instead of with stomach-churning anxiety? Was it because he was an artist, representing all that she had learned to mistrust in a man? Or was it because he just happened to be dangerously attractive? A bit of both, she decided. Unconsciously, she scrubbed the back of her hand across her lips as if to erase any trace of his kiss this morning. 'What will you tell Mum?' she asked by way of distraction.

'Just what I've told you—that I'm not cut out for the academic life. Don't look so worried, Carrie. I've got some money saved up from the allowance Mum sent me. It will keep me until I can make my first sales.'

'And if you don't sell anything?'

Krys's shoulders lifted carelessly. 'Then I'll have to go on the dole, won't I?'

Sensing her sister's disapproval, Krys tensed, her features setting. 'I know you think I should die before I go on the dole, but I think it's an even bigger shame to waste one's life doing less than the best that's in you. I'm capable of being a successful artist, I know I am. And if it means accepting handouts to achieve it, that's what I'll have to do.'

Carrie looked at her in disbelief. Krys had always been headstrong and impulsive, but this was too much. 'You sound like you don't care what I think,' she whispered.

'Frankly, I don't. Can't you see, Carrie, I can't *afford* to care if I'm to make it in my chosen career. If I let you influence me, I'll go meekly back to university and qualify as a teacher and I'll end up like . . . like . . .' She tailed off, her eyes round.

Carrie knew perfectly well why she couldn't go on. 'Like me,' she finished quietly. 'Working long hours at a job which will always be second best to me. That's what you were going to say, wasn't it?'

Awkwardly, Krys scuffed one shoe against the other. 'I don't want to hurt you, Carrie, but I wish you'd see things my way just for once.'

Where had she heard that before? Then it came back to her: Oscar Doyle had said much the same thing to their mother before he left home for good. 'You sound more like our father every day,' she observed tightly, trying to choke back her dismay.

'If I am, I'm proud of it!' Krys flung at her and stalked out of the room, slamming her bedroom door behind her.

More slowly, Carrie made her way to her own bedroom, the pressure of her whirling thoughts making her head ache. If only Krys knew how their mother had suffered at Oscar's hands she would realise the risk she was taking. But she'd been protected from most of the hardships, first by their mother, then by Carrie, so to her their father was a heroic figure whose family didn't understand him. Blood will out, she thought miserably, and there was nothing she could do to stop it.

'Why should you want to?' Roger asked when she said much the same thing to him over pre-dinner drinks on Saturday night.

'I don't want her making the same mistakes,' she said lamely.

'Nobody can learn from another's mistakes—only from their own.'

'I suppose you think mine is in trying to protect her?' she threw at him.

He took a sip of his Scotch and soda before he looked at her mildly. 'I wouldn't presume to tell you your mistakes.'

She got the message. Similarly, she should stay out of Krys's life. She compressed her lips into a thin line to keep from snapping back at him. How could a man like him understand what it was like to be part of a family, protecting and helping one another? 'Do you have any brothers or sisters?' she asked.

'No, I'm an only child. But before you ask how I can know what goes on between siblings, I should point out that my mother raised half a dozen foster children while I was growing up so I'm not entirely ignorant of family life.'

'I see,' she said, chastened. 'Does your family live in Sydney?'

He accepted the change of subject with good grace. 'No. I grew up in a coastal fishing village just north of Kempsey, in banana-growing country. My father was a local bank manager. He died two years ago and my mother moved over to Perth to live with her sister.'

'I'm sorry,' she murmured.

'Don't be. Dad and I were never close. He had . . . other career plans for me.'

Which explained his empathy with Krys. Suddenly restless, she jumped up. 'I'd better see to dinner, then you can look at the drawings Krys left for you.'

He caught at her hand and pulled her down on to the couch beside him. Off balance, she rolled against him and jerked herself upright. 'What's your hurry? he enquired. 'I thought Saturday was the one night when you working girls could let your hair down.'

'It is usually,' she agreed, caught off-guard by his sudden closeness and hating the way her breathing automatically quickened in response. 'But today was rather tiresome and I was planning an early night.'

'Is that an invitation?' he asked softly. When her startled gaze met his, she saw by his expression that he was teasing her.

'Very funny,' she said acidly. 'I suppose you were one of the people in favour of extending shopping hours on Friday nights and Saturdays?'

'Since most other civilised countries have them, I was,' he admitted. 'I didn't think of what it would be like for the people who worked in the stores. I expected they would hire extra staff or something.'

She shuffled sideways a little, trying discreetly to put

a bit more space between them. 'Most stores do,' she explained, 'but management are expected to work longer hours than the sales assistants, and we don't always get paid for the extra time.'

'I see. And you're management?'

'Yes, I am.'

He rested a hand on her knee for a moment then removed it before she could react. 'Don't sound so defensive. I wasn't trying to put you down.'

'Weren't you?' she demanded, her anger flaring. 'You've done nothing else since we met.'

He leaned forwards, resting muscular forearms on his knees, and stared into the drink he cradled in both hands. Their relative postures gave the illusion of greater distance between them and she felt her pulses slowing. 'If I did, it was in self-defence,' he explained. 'You were the one who tagged me as gay on the strength of a book jacket photo.'

Glad that he couldn't see the colour that flooded her cheeks at the reminder, she dropped her head. 'A theory you very quickly disproved, if I recall!'

The caressing gaze he directed at her told her he remembered every detail of the stolen kiss as vividly as she did. 'A kiss needn't prove anything,' he said languidly, but she wasn't deceived by his apparent disinterest. 'I can offer you much more proof if you want me to.'

'I'm sure you can,' she said as lightly as her constricting vocal chords allowed. 'But it's time I served our first course—and it isn't me!'

She was sure she heard him murmur, 'Pity,' as she fled to the safety of the kitchen.

Not knowing his tastes, she'd kept to safe choices with the menu. For a starter, there was asparagus vol au vent, followed by whole grilled John Dory in lemon butter, then strawberries marinaded in liqueur for dessert. After working for most of the day, of necessity the meal had to be simple, but she found herself hoping he would be impressed.

He was, returning for second helpings when invited, and cleaning his plate of all but the fine bones of the John Dory.

'That was damned marvellous . . . I mean, terrific,' he amended hastily.

Carrie was foolishly touched that he remembered her feelings about bad language. 'I'm glad you enjoyed it,' she said as she poured Cointreau into liqueur glasses to go with the coffee that was perking in the kitchen. She liked cooking, and it was pleasant to have an appreciative guest.

She accepted his offer of help in clearing the table. They stacked the dishes in the sink to wash later, then took their coffee and liqueurs into the living-room. In his slim, maroon cord jeans and open-necked white shirt, Roger looked completely at ease as he draped himself over the couch. Knowing he was watching her every move made her nervous and she spilled coffee into his saucer. 'I'm sorry, I'll get a cloth and wipe it up,' she volunteered.

He took the cup from her grasp and put it back on the tray. 'I have a better idea. Why don't you sit down and relax? You're like a cat on hot coals tonight. Either you're the nervous type—or I disturb you for some reason.'

Since she hated to admit that his presence was making her awkward, she shrugged. 'I must be the nervous type.'

'A bit sudden, isn't it?'

'What do you mean?'

'A store like Petrie's wouldn't entrust a large

department to a Nervous Nellie, now would they?'
When she didn't answer, he went on. 'Of course they
wouldn't. Which means for some reason, I make you
nervous. Why would that be, I wonder? It couldn't be
because of a simple kiss behind the filing cabinet, could
it?'

'Do you have to go on and on about it?' she
demanded hotly. 'You make it sound as if it mattered.'

'It did to me,' he said quietly. 'I already like you a lot,
Ms Doyle, and I have a hunch you feel the same spark
of interest.'

'That's absurd. We hardly know each other.'

He tilted one winged eyebrow at her. 'A situation I'd
like to change. I'm not often wrong about people.'

Remembering with a rush, she hung her head. 'I can
hardly say the same where you're concerned.'

He chuckled. 'Our first meeting was a bit bizarre.
But I can explain about that.'

'I've already told you that you don't owe me any
explanation.'

He reached for her hand, warming it in his. 'I think I
do if I'm to change your first impression of me as a
ne'er-do-well.'

'I didn't . . .'

He dismissed her denial with a gesture. 'Yes, you did.
Who wouldn't? I did turn up in your office unshaven,
bleary-eyed and swaying on my feet from lack of sleep.
Have you ever heard of the Asur River?'

Mystified, she shook her head.

'It's a river on the very rim of Indonesia, along the
border between Papua and Indonesia.' Roger's eyes
clouded with enthusiastic memories. 'You should see it,
Carrie. It's like the world before the coming of man—
all jungle, swamp and savannah woodland, a crocodile-
infested frontier. You can hear them splashing through

the shallows, then galloping away as your canoe glides up to their mud wallows.'

Involuntarily, she shuddered. 'It doesn't sound very pleasant!'

'It wasn't, but not because of the wildlife. What I didn't count on was running foul of the border patrols who mistook us for mercenaries and started shooting at us. Luckily neither my guide nor I was hurt, but we got out of there as fast as we could, leaving all our supplies and equipment behind.'

Light was beginning to dawn. 'All your clothes were left behind?'

'My travellers' cheques, personal gear, everything. Luckily I had my passport and ticket on me so I was able to catch the first plane back to Australia. I planned to get some rest and a change of clothes before I came in to see you but I was so jet-lagged and exhausted that I couldn't sleep. I didn't really know what I was doing when I turned up in your office.'

'Couldn't you have gone home rather than to a hotel when you reached Sydney?' she asked.

'I've been travelling around so much in the last year or so that most of my possessions were in storage, so I couldn't get at them until I'd been back a few days. I should have postponed my appointment with you but I wasn't thinking straight.'

'What were you doing in New Guinea?' she asked suddenly.

He looked away. 'Exploring, just looking around.'

Carrie had the uncomfortable feeling that he wasn't being wholly honest with her. 'Are you a spy?' she challenged him.

His laughter was too quick to be anything but genuine. 'Good grief, no. The guards were just trigger-happy. They didn't stop to ask who we were before they started shooting.'

She still felt uneasy about his explanation. Oh, sure, it explained why he had looked so terrible when he first came into her office. But instead of reassuring her, he had only confirmed her worst fears. He was every bit as irresponsible as her father had been, rushing in where angels knew better than to tread. Men like Oscar and Roger could see no harm in exploring along an unstable border and never gave a thought to the trouble they caused, nor the anguish they inflicted on the people waiting for them at home.

Roger watched the interplay of emotions on her face. 'You still don't approve of me, do you? Now you're freezing me out because I don't fit into your mould.'

Her eyes flashed defensive fire. 'You're wrong!'

'Am I? You reacted the same way to my story as you do whenever your father is mentioned, and I think I know why. I think you're afraid, Carrie Doyle!'

Shaken, she gulped her liqueur then set the glass down. 'I'm not afraid of you—or my father!'

'I didn't say you were. You're afraid of yourself, because you know you possess the same adventurous streak and you're terrified that one day you won't be able to stop yourself kicking over the traces and doing something crazy—like exploring a wild and dangerous river just because it's there.'

His words affected her more strongly than she allowed him to see. How often had she expressed the same fears to herself? 'The fact remains that I don't desert my responsibilities and go off into the wilds,' she said stiffly.

His features relaxed into a teasing smile. 'So, you admit that the idea has crossed your mind once or twice?'

He was impossible! 'Once or twice,' she admitted reluctantly, her tone subdued. Anxious to end this conversation, she stood up. 'Hadn't you better take a look at Krys's drawings, since it was what you came for?'

He uncoiled himself from the sofa with seeming reluctance. 'Maybe it was why you invited me, but it wasn't the reason I came,' he said softly, his mouth alarmingly near to her ear.

Her eyes refused to meet his and she took a sudden, passionate interest in the patterned wallpaper. 'It . . . it wasn't?'

The touch of his hands on her shoulders jarred her with the suddenness of a lift jolting to a stop. She had barely recovered from the shock of the contact when she felt herself being drawn backwards against him until her spine was pressed against his chest and her thighs were cushioned against his.

Common sense told her to pull away and lead the way to Krys's room, but the way she felt had nothing to do with sense and everything to do with sensation.

Her pulses throbbed and heat surged through her body. 'No, Roger,' she whispered, but feebly and without conviction.

Very slowly, he bent his head and grazed the sensitive back of her neck with his lips, sending shivers of desire all the way down her spine. 'What did you say?' he murmured, his mouth resting on her neck.

'I said . . . oh, Roger!' She hadn't meant the groan of pleasure to escape but as she framed a repeat of her denial, he nuzzled her hair away from her neck and continued to leave a trail of kisses along her hairline. His breath was a fiery wind, ruffling her hair.

If they had been facing each other it would have cost her a lot not to kiss him back. But standing spoon fashion, there was nothing for her to do but surrender to the torrent of sensations his nuzzling explorations aroused in her. Unconsciously, she arched her shoulders back, seeking even closer contact with him while her hands fluttered upwards to caress the back of his bent head.

Suddenly she became aware of an insistent pressure against the small of her back and her feet moved automatically forwards, carrying her in the direction she gradually realised he meant her to take. As one they were moving towards her bedroom door.

This time she found the strength to twist free of him and move a short distance away, her breath coming in strained gasps. 'No, Roger; I told you I wasn't on the menu tonight.'

Unperturbed, he smoothed his hair back where her caresses had ruffled it. 'That may be what you said, but your actions just now gave me a different impression.'

'I seem fated to lose all sense of self-control when you're around,' she exclaimed.

'I told you we're made for each other,' he said, his tone light and teasing again as he also regained control of rampant emotions. 'We could be very good for each other, you and I, if you'll give me half a chance.'

She'd just given him a lot more than that and look where it very nearly led! Despondently, she slumped against the wall. 'It's no use, it wouldn't work.'

'Why? Because I'm an itinerant artist living in a hotel?'

She had been about to say it was because he was dangerously attractive. In time, she stopped herself. If he found out how she felt he wouldn't give up so readily. Better let him think her resistance was fuelled entirely by her prejudice against cartoonists. 'Just because, that's all.'

His eyes, which moments before had been aglow with passion for her, now held battle lights. 'So, you're determined to hold your stupid prejudice against me, are you?'

Instantly she was on the defensive. 'It isn't stupid! The . . . the other would have been stupid, since I know what sort of future is ahead of me if I encourage you. I've had years of watching my mother suffer to teach me what life is like with men like you.'

'Of all the pig-headed——'

Before he could finish, she flung open the door to Krys's bedroom which also doubled as a studio. 'I think you'll find everything you need in here,' she said, keeping her voice steady with an effort.

His answering look was filled with irony. 'I doubt it, but I'll take a look at the pictures anyway.'

Considering how close they had just come to making love, his changed mood as he approached Krys's drawings was a shock for Carrie. Even though she was the one who had rejected him, she felt shut out as he moved from sketch to sketch, appraising them carefully and silently.

She watched him for a few minutes then returned to the living-room where she began to clear away the coffee things.

Try as she might to banish it, the feel of Roger's lips against the back of her neck persisted in sending shivers of longing down her spine. The memory of how willingly she had taken those few faltering steps towards the bedroom remained to disturb her. Surely it was much too soon for him to have such an effect on her?

Why did it have to be him, of all men, who affected her so? Why couldn't he have been a banker or a train driver, anything but the one breed of man she could never trust herself to?

She was elbow deep in soapy dishwater, wrestling with her thoughts, when Roger came back into the room. Even before any sound betrayed his presence, she was aware of him. Shaking the suds off her hands, she turned towards him. 'Well?'

One look at his set expression gave her an answer. 'You aren't going to discourage her, are you?'

'No, I'm not. As a matter of fact, I'm going to recommend her to some gallery owners I know, one of whom specialises in black and white line work.'

Tears of frustration pricked at her eyes, mingling with the steam from the washing-up water, and Carrie dried her hands impatiently, swabbing her face before he could see her dewy eyes. 'I hope you realise you're destroying a young girl's life by doing this?'

'You're wrong. Krys has talent, real talent. You're just so prejudiced against her choice of career that you won't face it. If you stand in her way, you'll be the one destroying her life, not me.'

'She can have a career and still draw as well, can't she?'

His lips narrowed into a tight line of annoyance. 'You won't accept that art is a career, will you? My God, you remind me of my father.'

Although she didn't know in what way she resembled his father, she sensed that it wasn't a compliment. She flinched at his derisive tone, finding that she craved his approval more than she would have thought possible. She clasped her hands in a gesture of supplication. 'I know I'm doing this all wrong, but I only want what's best for Krys.'

'For Krys or yourself?' he demanded.

'Hardly for myself. I couldn't have the life I wanted and it's too late for me to go back and start again now, but it isn't too late for Krys.'

His steady gaze bored into her accusingly. 'You really believe all that noble rubbish, don't you? Can't you see, Carrie, you're censuring your sister for doing something you'd half like to do yourself, given the chance?'

Startled, she blinked hard. 'Me? But I'm not artistic like Krys.'

'No? Then what do you call those book displays you labour so lovingly over at Petrie's? Or the arrangement of our dinner tonight, which was pure poetry? I think you're coming down so hard on Krys to stop yourself looking too closely at your own needs and desires—which may not turn out to be so different from hers.'

She felt as if he had stripped her naked and left her standing defenceless in the centre of the kitchen. It was an effort not to spread her hands to cover what felt like her exposed body. How could anyone see so deeply into her very soul? It couldn't be true; she wouldn't even consider it. 'I think you'd better go,' she said flatly.

He was unperturbed. 'Have it your way for now. But I warn you, I'm not giving up on Krys. For that matter, I'm not giving up on you, either. I like you a hell of a lot and I'm determined to lure you down off that pedestal of yours long enough for us to get to know each other properly. It can get very cold and lonely up there, sweetheart.'

Far from sounding affectionate, the term of endearment only emphasised the gulf which had opened up between them and which seemed to be widening before her eyes. Silently, she led the way to the front door and held it open for him.

At first she thought he was going to leave with only a

cursory 'good night'. Just as she began to close the door on him, he blocked it with his foot.

Leaning through the opening, he kissed her quickly on the mouth. 'Thanks for dinner. I meant what I said. I'll be in touch.' Then he was gone.

The kiss had been no more than a fleeting touch of his lips to hers, but she was devastated by its impact. She had never felt more alone than she did after she had closed the door on him and stood leaning against it, her hands pressed to her burning cheeks.

It made no sense. Tonight he had told her truths about herself she wouldn't have endured from anyone else. Then he had said he wanted to see her again and would be in touch.

The crazy part was, she wanted him to.

CHAPTER FOUR

THE phone rang and Carrie reached for it but was forestalled by Helen. 'I'm quite capable of answering a phone, thanks,' she said, giving Carrie a look of irritation.

It was Carrie's cue to find something useful to do but despite herself, she couldn't walk away until Helen's words made it clear it wasn't Roger calling.

What was the matter with her? She had been like a cat on hot bricks since Saturday night when Roger said he would get in touch with her. She presumed this meant he would telephone, but when half the week went by without a word from him, she began to wonder if she had misunderstood. It was bad enough that she seized the phone before Helen could move, but when Carrie began to eavesdrop on her boss's conversations, Helen looked at her as if she had lost her marbles.

Maybe she had. She had never felt like this about a man before, far less one she had known as briefly as Roger. One business meeting, an ill-fated dinner *à trois* and a meal at her place hardly added up to a passionate romance. Yet there was the kiss in Helen's office, so brief, yet so compelling that even now she could feel its imprint on her lips. Equally vivid was the memory of the desire she had experienced in his arms, and she wondered if he was right. Maybe there was such a thing as falling in love across a crowded room.

If only she didn't know his type so well. It was bad enough that he shared the same profession as her father. Add that to his obvious wanderlust, evidenced

by the New Guinea episode, and now his failure to call.
It was as if she was being warned against him with
every move he made.

She became aware of a hand tugging insistently at
her elbow. 'I said, is anyone serving in this
department?'

Her vision cleared and she looked into the irate face
of a woman holding a handful of books from the
bargain table. She forced herself to smile. 'I'm sorry,
madam. I can help you with those. Please come this
way.'

The woman snorted loudly, annoyed at having the
rest of her complaint cut short by Carrie's smiling
apology. At the cash register, Carrie registered the sale
and handed the wrapped books to the woman with a
smile. 'Have a nice day.'

Accepting the parcel, the woman gestured towards
the poster of Roger that looked down at them from
above a display of his books. 'When's he due here?'

The details of the signing session were clearly printed
on the poster but Carrie restrained herself. Perhaps the
woman was short-sighted. Besides, she knew the day
and time off by heart. 'This Friday at eleven.'

The woman frowned. 'Hmmph. I may come in for
his autograph—for my nephew, you understand. But I
won't be buying any books.'

Carrie forced a smile. 'That's all right, madam, a
purchase is not required.'

As the woman stumped off, Helen came up to
Carrie.'Were you expecting a call from Roger Torkan?'

Carrie's eyes flew wide and she took a half-step
towards the office when Helen touched her arm. 'He
rang off. I told him you were with a customer.'

Trying to conceal her disappointment, Carrie busied

herself with sorting some sales slips. 'I see. What did he want?'

'He didn't leave any message but said he would see you here on Friday.' Helen turned towards her office then thought better of it and loked keenly at Carrie. 'Maybe now I'll get to answer my own phone for a while!'

So that Helen wouldn't see her sudden rush of colour, Carrie decided that now was as good a time as any to tidy the bargain tables. Helen watched her silently for a few minutes then went back into her office.

Why had Roger picked just that moment to call? Another few seconds and she would have been free to talk to him. What had he wanted? It couldn't have been a date or he would have called again instead of saying he would see her on Friday.

What a fool she was, reading so much into a couple of brief encounters! Granted, they had struck sparks off each other every time, but they were mostly sparks of antagonism. Enough to suggest that any closer relationship between them would be a stormy one.

Her hands full of books, she exhaled slowly. It was all too confusing. One moment she had her life nicely sorted out, and the next she was torn in two by this crazy attraction for a man who was completely unsuitable for her. Why couldn't he have been gay after all? It would have solved everything.

Seeing him in the store on Friday was enough to dispel any such notion. By the advertised time, several hundred people had crowded into the book department. Most were women, and Carrie couldn't help wondering how much of their interest was in the man rather than his work.

As it happened, she wasn't there when he arrived. She was so obviously on tenterhooks that Helen, in exasperation, sent her to the receiving room to check a new shipment of books. Unfortunately, a number of the crates held stocks of Roger's book, so she was constantly confronted by his smiling face on the dust jackets, mocking her as she ticked off each consignment.

'That's the last of them, love,' the manager of the receiving room assured her as she signed the sheaf of documents he proffered.

'You won't waste any time getting them up to us, will you?' she asked him. 'With Rog ... with the author making a personal appearance, there's bound to be a demand for these.'

The man winked at her. 'No worries. They're as good as on the shelves.'

Freed at last from the tedious task, she hurried to the staff lift and punched in the number of her floor. She told herself that it was knowing she was needed to cope with the crowd, rather than eagerness to see Roger again, that made her heart race so disturbingly.

Her flushed face looked back at her from the lift's mirrored wall, the eyes accusing. 'In a pig's eye,' the expression told her.

At the sight of him seated at a desk on the raised platform in the middle of the department, she almost fled back to the receiving rom. He looked heart-stoppingly vital as he sat forward, his ankles hooked around the chair legs as he signed the books his fans thrust forward. An overhead spotlight gave his hair enticing highlights, and the shadow of his bent head created a suggestion of the straw-coloured stubble on his chin she remembered so vividly from their first encounter. He presented an overwhelmingly masculine picture. How could she ever have mistaken it for anything else?

At a sharp word from Helen who was beseiged by customers at the cash register, Carrie waded into the throng, accepting money and wrapping books as fast as she could.

Roger was oblivious of her presence, but she was achingly conscious of his and kept darting furtive glances at him over her shoulder, almost as if to assure herself he was really here.

'I can handle this now. You see how much longer Roger wants to keep going,' Helen breathed into her ear.

Carrie glanced at her boss's face but it was impassive. If Helen sensed how eager Carrie was to speak to Roger, she didn't show it. 'Thanks,' she said breathlessly.

As she approached the dais, Roger saw her for the first time. His intensely blue eyes bored into her like gimlets. 'I thought you weren't coming,' he mouthed, as he signed yet another book.

A forward-thrust book collided with Carrie's mid-section and she looked down in annoyance which changed to compassion as she met the pleading eyes of a very small lady. Her arm wasn't long enough to place the book on Roger's table. 'Could you?' she asked sweetly.

Carrie took the book. 'Your name?'

'Caroline Crossrow. You're very kind.'

Carrie handed the book up to Roger. 'Could you sign this for Caroline, please?' She was sure Roger couldn't see the diminutive woman from over his desk.

His eyes sparkled with amusement. 'Naturally.'

He wrote busily, and when he handed the book back, Carrie glanced automatically at the dedication then froze in dismay. It said, 'To Caroline, for a special night at your place, and hopes of more to come.'

She could feel her face suffusing with colour. 'Not me!' she hissed. 'This lady, Caroline Crossrow.'

Rising, he peered over the desk. Then in a smooth movement, he swept another book from the pile on his desk and autographed it with a flourish, passing it to Carrie when he was finished. This time the dedication was a harmless, 'For Caroline—laugh and the world laughs with you. Love, Roger Torkan.' She handed it to the woman waiting expectantly beside her. After reading the inscription, she hugged the book to her. 'It's beautiful. Thank you so much.'

'My pleasure. Have a nice day, Caroline.' His velvety voice must have been all that Caroline Crossrow absorbed from where she stood but she went away glowing with pleasure.

'You shouldn't have done that,' Carrie said to Roger when there was a temporary respite.

'I shouldn't have given her my autograph?' he asked innocently.

'You know what I mean. I'll have to keep this book now.'

'That was the general idea.'

'No, I mean I'll have to pay for it, since it came out of stock.'

He shook his head. 'Uh-uh. I brought some copies with me so I could give a few away if I felt like it. And I felt like it.'

For an irrational moment, she felt like imitating Caroline Crossrow and hugging the autographed book to her. Despite their disagreement over Krys, he thought the evening at her place had been 'a special night', did he? The discovery that he was looking forward to more of them was alarming, since common sense told her not to get involved with him at all.

Nevertheless, the idea made her feel curiously warm and cherished.

Moments later, however, the feeling was dispelled by the arrival of Bianca West. The woman had obviously gone to a lot of trouble to dress up for the occasion. Already beautiful, she looked sensational in a two-piece peplum suit of amber shot silk. Her height was emphasised with the slimmest of stiletto heels and her elegant page-boy hairstyle had definitely not been slept in.

Bianca eyed Carrie with distaste then turned a brilliant smile on Roger. 'I don't believe we've met.'

Recognising her cue, Carrie said, 'This is one of our best customers, Bianca West. Bianca, Roger Torkan.'

Bianca held out a graceful hand. 'I'm thrilled to meet you . . . Roger. I buy the *Examiner* every day so I won't miss a word of "The Many Loves of Emily".'

'It's kind of you to say so,' Roger mumbled, taken aback by the obvious flattery.

'No, no, I mean it. I think your Emily is the most entertaining feature in the whole paper.' She leaned forward conspiratorially. 'Tell me, though. Do you base Emily's . . . ah . . . exploits on your own *affaires de coeur*?'

Carrie might have become invisible, so concentrated was Roger's gaze on Bianca. He laughed throatily. 'Hardly, since Emily is female and I'm male.'

Bianca almost purred. 'I *had* noticed.'

Feeling faintly ill, Carrie stepped down off the dais and backed away, not wanting to hear any more of the exchange. Couldn't Roger see what a predatory female Bianca was? Her . . . ah . . . exploits were well documented in the social columns around town. The only thing keeping her respectable was her vast inherited fortune, which she shared generously enough with charity to be forgiven most indiscretions. Roger must have heard of her, surely?

He was as bad as her father. The thought came unbidden into Carrie's mind. He had been just as blind when it came to women.

Shaken, Carrie went back to the cash register and relieved Helen. Maybe Bianca's arrival was a timely warning. The sexual attraction, the inscription in the book ... they weren't enough compensation for a lifetime of misery such as her mother had endured, and she would do well to remember it.

By lunch-time, the rush petered out and Roger was corralled by a journalist from a women's magazine. She had arranged with Helen to interview Roger in the office.

Since Carrie's home-made sandwich was in her handbag in Helen's office, she couldn't retrieve it either to put Roger's book away or go to lunch until the interview was over.

'When you go, take an extra half-hour to make up for not having your coffee break this morning,' Helen told her. She gestured towards the closed glass door of the office. 'It looks like they're finishing now so you can get your things.'

As she spoke, the journalist emerged, stowing a notebook and miniature tape recorder into her briefcase. She stopped to talk to Helen, and Carrie slipped into the office where Roger was shrugging on a sports jacket.

He noticed her before she could slip out again and he reached for her arm. 'Off to lunch?'

She nodded, uncomfortably aware of the warmth of his hand through the thin material of her dress.

'Join me?'

'No, I . . . I only have an hour. It isn't long enough to go out anywhere.'

'Liar! I checked with your boss and she says you didn't have a break this morning so she was going to let you make it up now.'

Could Helen possibly be matchmaking? It seemed unlikely, so it had to be coincidence that she had extended Carrie's break just when Roger wanted to take her out. 'It was nice of Helen,' she said awkwardly.

'No more than your due. You were working damned hard this morning.'

'So were you,' she said sincerely.

He shrugged. 'Signing books is hardly work.' He flexed his fingers. 'Although it is hard on the hand. I wonder how politicians survive all that handshaking.'

A streak of devilment made her say, 'Oh, Mr Torkan, you have such masculine hands. Are they the ones you use to draw with?'

It was such a wicked imitation of Bianca West's breathless tones that he laughed then looked at her keenly. 'Could it be that you were bothered by the attention I was paying to Miss West?'

She draped her handbag strap over her shoulder. 'Why should I be bothered? If you choose to chat her up, that's your business.'

'I'd say it was the other way around, wouldn't you? She was the one doing most of the chatting.'

There was nothing she could say without confirming his accusation that she was jealous, so she led the way out of the office and back to the lift. Roger elected to accompany her out of the staff entrance.

'If the staff leave by the front door we're suspected of taking half the store with us,' she explained.

'Nothing like it. Only one copy of a book,' he reminded her, amusement in his tone.

Her pulse began to race. She had forgotten the autographed book in her handbag. What if the security people chose today to make one of their random checks? She could explain the presence of the book in her bag easily enough—Roger would vouch for it—but she would die if anyone read the inscription he had written inside.

Luckily, the guard passed her through with a friendly wave, and she breathed a sigh of relief when they reached the street.

'Don't tell me you were scared he would read the inscription in your book?' Roger said, divining her fears. 'I thought *Ms* Doyle wouldn't care what anyone thought.'

'You don't know Petrie's grapevine. They'd have us married off in no time.'

He rubbed his chin thoughtfully. 'Not a bad idea at that.'

'Oh, really!'

He couldn't know how hard she had fought for respectability ever since she was a child. It was bad enough being teased by your schoolmates because your father was a cartoonist, but when it meant you were too poor to afford basic school equipment, it was unendurable. It was another reason why she had been so appalled about Krys's choice of career.

Lost in thought, she let Roger lead her to a nearby bistro, no longer surprised when he ordered their meal from the French menu and dealt with it perfectly. Whatever Roger was inside, outwardly he had acquired an enviable veneer of respectability. If only it went deeper than that.

'How did your mother take Krys's decision?' he asked as they ate.

Her fork poised in mid-air, she hesitated. 'She wasn't happy about it . . .' she began.

'But the sky didn't fall down?' he anticipated.

She set the fork down slowly. 'Actually, she took it much better than I expected. She tried to talk Krys into staying on at university, of course, but when she realised her mind was made up, she said it was Krys's life.'

'But you're disappointed that she didn't back you up,' he stated rather than asked.

Angry now, she glared at him across the table, her appetite waning. 'I wasn't waiting to say "I told you so", if that's what you mean. But I thought Mum of all people would realise what Krys is letting herself in for.'

He was unmoved by her anger. 'She probably does. She's also wise enough to let Krys find out for herself.'

'You arty types are all alike,' she said bitterly. 'I should have known you'd side with Krys.'

'I'm not siding with anybody,' he said, developing a hard edge of impatience in his voice. 'I meant what I said in the book, Carrie. I want to see you again. My professional interest in Krys has nothing to do with you and me.'

It was out before she could stop herself. 'Then why didn't you leave a message when you rang, instead of leaving me dangling?'

He sat back, crumpling his napkin on to the table. 'So that's what all the antagonism is about! It isn't Krys at all. Because I didn't speak to you when I rang, I'm just as unreliable as your father and all artists, is that it?'

It was exactly what she had been thinking, and she looked away guiltily. 'You did say you'd be in touch,' she said in a small voice.

'I did and I was. Helen said you were with a customer and I didn't want to interrupt you. Besides, I have work to do too, despite what you think of we layabout arty types. 'Emily' doesn't draw herself.'

'I know, I'm sorry.'

'Then you'll go out with me again?'

For a few agonised moments, she toyed with the spoon in her saucer then dropped it, rattling the china. 'I don't know, Roger. I need some time.'

He signalled for their bill and paid for both of them, over her protests. 'Take all the time you want, as long as you reach the right decision.'

When he left her outside Petrie's staff entrance, he touched one hand to her chin, tilting her face upwards so she wondered if he was going to kiss her there in public. But he must have borne in mind her warning about the grapevine, because he merely brushed her lips with his fingers, in imitation of a kiss.

'You get in touch with me this time, huh?' he said. 'That way there won't be any misunderstandings!'

As Roger started to walk away, she felt an urgent need to restrain him for just a few moments longer. 'Wait, I . . . do I call you at the hotel?'

'That's where I'm based for the time being.'

With a last wave, he strode off, his broad back tantalising her as he melted into the crowd. He was based in a hotel for the time being. Where would he be next week or next month? Why should she find herself caring so much?

Next day, she awoke with a start to find the sun streaming into her bedroom. Just as she was about to bound out of bed, thinking she had slept through the alarm, she remembered that today was her half day. She wasn't due at the store until after lunch. Thankfully, she sank back against the pillows.

From the kitchen came the sound of clinking china. Could Krys actually be up and making coffee? Miraculous though it seemed, she was, and she came into Carrie's room carrying a steaming cup, the day's paper tucked under one arm.

'What brought this on?' asked Carrie suspiciously as she sipped the coffee.

'Oh ... nothing,' Krys said studiedly. 'I've been reading the paper in bed, and I thought you might like to do the same. Especially the comics.'

Now what was all that about? Carrie wondered as her sister left the room with alacrity. Usually if she wanted Carrie to notice a particular cartoon, it was thrust under her nose. This heavy hinting was something new. Curiously, she turned to the comics page.

As soon as she saw it, she understood Krys's reticence. Roger's strip, 'The Many Loves of Emily', leapt out at her from the page. For there, being welcomed as Emily's new flatmate, was a character identified as Lucy Trimble. And Lucy Trimble was Carrie to the life.

'How could he?' she asked aloud as she stared at the likeness. Knowing her dislike of cartoons, the wretched man had gone and drawn her into his strip for everyone to see. Reluctantly, she read the strip which took up a quarter of the newspaper page. Not being a regular reader, she had no idea of the storyline, but she kept returning to the likeness of herself. Lucy Trimble, indeed! What wouldn't she say to Roger Torkan when she got hold of him! She'd sue, that was what she'd do!

'On what grounds?' Krys asked her over breakfast. 'It's only a resemblance. It could be coincidence.'

'In a pig's eye!' Carrie retorted, remembering saying the same thing to her reflection in the staff lift. Then, she had been trying to deny her attraction to Roger. This was different. 'He had no right to use me as his model!'

'Who says he did? Just because Lucy has the same general look as you do, doesn't mean it's meant to be you. Lots of artists use real people as their inspiration. If it was me, I'd be flattered.'

Carrie didn't feel flattered. She felt used, and she wasn't looking forward to facing her fellow staff members at Petrie's either.

Most of them hadn't seen the morning papers when she went to work on Saturday afternoon, and Sunday was thankfully a holiday, but if Roger made Lucy a regular part of his strip, then she was in for a fearful ribbing on Monday.

Unfortunately, Roger wasn't at his hotel on the many occasions when she tried to reach him. Finally, the receptionist advised her that he had gone away on business for a few days. She tried the Central Coast number on his card but an answering machine informed her the number belonged to somebody called Gil Marten. He must take messages for Roger, but she didn't feel like spilling her frustrations out to a machine so she slammed the phone down. What was she to do now?

By Thursday, she still hadn't caught up with Roger, and by then, Lucy had much more to complain about. In the comic strip, she had hired an interior decorator called Harvey to work on Emily's flat, and the poor man had fallen hopelessly in love with her.

As Carrie continued to read the daily strip in awful fascination, Lucy rejected the man repeatedly until by Friday, he was standing on a ledge outside Lucy's window, threatening to jump unless she took pity on him.

Finally, Carrie could stand it no longer and decided to call at Roger's hotel address on her way home. He couldn't stay out of town for ever, and *someone* was drawing the work she was reading in the paper each day.

The hotel receptionist gave her directions to Roger's room on the eighth floor. He confirmed that Roger had returned that day and offered to announce her arrival. 'No, thanks, I'll surprise him,' she said grimly. She ignored the clerk's speculative looks and headed for the lift.

'Come in, it isn't locked,' Roger's voice responded to her knock. When she let herself in, she found him bent over a drawing board angled near the window, sticking some grey background tones on to a piece of artwork. At his feet was a snowstorm of paper fragments and there was a pen wedged behind his ear. He kept working, saying over his shoulder, 'Put the coffee on the bedside table, thanks, dear.'

An unwonted thrill coursed through her at the sight of him, so engrossed in his work but she forced herself to remember her mission. 'Don't you "dear" me, you villain!' she fumed.

Startled, he looked up at last. 'Carrie! I'm sorry, I thought you were room service. This is a surprise!'

'Not as big as the one I got, finding you'd drawn me into your rotten comic strip without a by-your-leave.'

He looked genuinely bewildered. 'Whatever I'm supposed to have done . . .'

'There's no supposed about it! It's bad enough that your Lucy Trimble character looks like me. Now she's embroiled in this ridiculous love affair with her decorator, who bears a curious resemblance to Roger Torkan!'

He chuckled, the sound sending more goose bumps down her spine, which she grimly ignored. 'I didn't know you were such a fan.'

'I don't have a choice if I want to find out what I'm

supposedly doing each day. You may think this is a clever way of winning me over but I'm telling you now, you can jump off your window ledge for all I care.'

He caught on in a rush, or else he was a superb actor. 'Oh, you must mean Friday's "Emily" strip. Sorry, Harvey can't jump yet. His threat is the cliff-hanger which keeps the readers around until Monday.'

She refused to be impressed. 'It may work for your readers, but it isn't going to work with me . . . Harvey.'

There was a long silence before he spoke again, then his tone was noticeably cooler. 'Who says it's supposed to?'

'But I thought . . .'

'You could have thought wrong, you know. Have you considered you're reading too much into a harmless cartoon?'

It was exactly what Krys had suggested and Carrie wondered if she was being foolish. She had been so sure that 'Lucy' was meant to be her, she had refused to consider anything else. 'You've got to admit that Lucy does look like me,' she ventured diffidently.

'I often take my inspiration from real life,' he explained, again echoing Krys. 'Do you mind very much?'

'I suppose not.' She was ashamed to tell him of her earlier dread that her workmates would tease her. In fact, Krys was the only one who had noticed the resemblance.

'Then there is hope for me?' he asked, his tone brightening.'

'I don't know. We don't seem to be good for each other.'

'I'll be the judge of what's good for me,' he said evenly. 'So speak for yourself.'

'I'm not even doing a good job of that,' she said

miserably. Why couldn't she make up her mind? She had been sure she shouldn't see him again, so why couldn't she say goodbye and be done with it?

He forestalled her. 'What are you doing this weekend?'

Luckily, she had an answer ready. 'Visiting my mother. In the Blue Mountains. Alone.'

Why she added this last, she didn't know, unless it was to discourage him from offering to go with her. 'Sounds cosy,' he agreed, not sounding in the least put out. 'Will you call me when you get back on Monday?'

He didn't give up easily, she thought with a sinking heart. 'All right,' she heard herself agreeing.

Built at the end of last century, Megalong was a grand old place perched on one of the great cliffs which overlooked the Megalong Valley.

Normally, she would have enjoyed a weekend of helping her mother run the guesthouse and taking long walks in the crisp mountain air when things were quiet. But this weekend, her thoughts kept turning back to Roger. What was he doing alone in Sydney? Come to that, was he alone? The very idea that he might not be tormented her.

During the weekend, only half of her attention was on the conversations she had with her mother, so she was startled to discover half-way through one that Kay was considering selling Megalong because running costs were getting out of hand.

Her mother had accepted the idea calmly, but Carrie was troubled by the thought of losing the only roots she knew. Kay had brushed aside Carrie's suggestion that she ask Oscar for help. After all, if he had been a better provider, Kay wouldn't be in this fix now. But her mother insisted she would solve the problem alone.

So it was in a mood of frustration that Carrie kissed her goodbye and caught her train back to Sydney. She looked around restlessly, wishing she had thought to buy a paperback at Katoomba station.

A chuckling sound across the aisle drew her attention. Seeing her questioning look, the matronly woman in the seat opposite wiped her eyes and smiled apologetically. 'I shouldn't read this in public,' she explained, gesturing towards her paper, 'but this Emily is just so funny. I have a daughter like her, you know.'

'That's nice,' Carrie said non-committally. It would be too coincidental if the woman was reading Roger's strip. 'I haven't seen today's paper.'

The woman offered Carrie her crumpled newspaper. 'Be my guest. I get off at the next stop, but I know what it's like to miss an episode.' She leaned across the aisle. 'I'll bet Harvey wins Lucy over in the end.'

Want to bet? Carrie thought cynically, but kept it to herself. Until now, she'd hardly considered the millions of readers Roger must have, or his effect on their lives. Foolishly, she'd been thinking of the strip as a sort of private communication between them. 'What do you think Lucy ought to do?' she asked suddenly.

Without hesitation, the woman said, 'Give him a chance, that's all. My daughter kept a good man dangling like that—in a manner of speaking, I mean. And she lost him in the end. Lucy will do the same if she isn't careful.' Bidding Carrie a cheerful good day, she gathered her belongings and left the train at the next station.

Alone with the newspaper and with the woman's advice burning in her ears, Carrie turned unwillingly to the cartoon page.

This time, Emily was telling a neighbour that Lucy had gone away for a few days. Harvey, the hapless decorator, was still clinging to his window ledge high above the city, and refused to come in until Lucy returned. Why didn't Lucy come back and put the poor man out of his misery? Carrie wondered, then realised what she was thinking. Damn Roger—he had managed to make her feel sorry for Harvey while wishing that Lucy was less hard-hearted!

Although she told herself the cartoon strip had nothing to do with real life, she couldn't help wondering what Roger was trying to tell her. Was he using Harvey and Lucy to tell Carrie he was out on a limb because she wouldn't go out with him?

There was one way to find out and that was to call and make a date with him. What happened to Harvey next would prove her theory one way or the other.

All the same, she felt foolish when she got off the train at home, carrying the old newspaper. What if Lucy's love life went off in a completely different direction from her own? Carrie would be committed to going out with Roger against her better judgment, all because she had let herself be influenced by a stupid comic strip.

At all costs, she'd better make sure Krys never found out about her fears, or she would never hear the end of it.

CHAPTER FIVE

SHE needn't have worried. When she carried her
suitcase inside there was no sign of Krys. A note
propped up on the dining table said that Krys was
attending an art show and wouldn't be home until late
in the evening. 'Please don't wait up. I don't know what
time I'll be back,' the message ended.

After the hustle and bustle of Megalong with its
floating population of guests the flat felt lonely, so
Carrie switched on the television set, letting it chatter
in the background while she unpacked. At least it
provided company.

Having stowed her things away and put out a skirt
and blouse for work tomorrow, she made herself some
scrambled eggs and toast which she carried back to the
living-room to eat in front of the television set.

For once the room was neat and tidy. Either Krys
had made a special effort to tidy everything up before
Carrie returned, or she hadn't spent much time here
over the weekend. Though tempted to give Krys the
benefit of the doubt, Carrie knew her sister too well.
She must have been out all weekend. She grimaced.
Dropping out of university hadn't hurt Krys's social
life. Not that she had neglected her work prospects,
either. She had made the rounds of all the galleries
Roger had suggested, so far without any luck. But she
had plenty of time, Carrie thought loyally. Roger was
wrong about her attitude. She didn't want to say 'I told
you so'. No one would be more pleased to see Krys
succeed.

Suddenly, she sat forward, her eyes riveted on the televison screen. The news was on and the announcer was talking about a new exhibition by a famous wildlife artist, Gil Marten.

Carrie remembered the name. He was the man who took messages for Roger. More importantly though, she was sure they were talking about the art show Krys mentioned in her note. Carrie was afraid to go and check in case she missed the report. Maybe she would catch a glimpse of Krys.

It seemed unlikely as the camera panned across a packed room. An announcer droned on about the importance of the exhibiton, the proceeds from which were being donated to a wildlife preservation fund.

'The artist himself is here tonight, along with many other distinguished visitors including the Lord Mayor,' the announcer went on.

Carrie ignored all that, her eyes scanning for signs of Krys. There! She couldn't mistake that shining blonde head and bubbly personality anywhere, even in such a crowd.

'The little monster, she's pinched my dress!' breathed Carrie, half out of annoyance and half out of pride at seeing her sister on television. Then she forgot about Krys's borrowed finery as she saw who her sister's escort was. It was Roger.

The TV cameras, which could be so unkind at times, favoured him, emphasising the broad span of his shoulders and his bronzed complexion.

As the camera lingered on him almost lovingly, Krys said something to him and he laughed down at her in a way which sent shafts of pain through Carrie's chest.

The picture dissolved to a pen of cattle and a farmer being interviewed about Australia's animal quarantine regulations. Carrie stared at it dumbly for a moment, before reaching to snap it off. Roger hadn't waited long before finding someone else to share his weekend.

It was her own fault, she was the first to admit. But she hadn't expected it to hurt as much as this. She tried to tell herself she was distressed for Krys's sake. He was not only years too old for her sister, but the same objections held true for Krys as for Carrie. He was a reckless adventurer with no fixed address or steady income, and now he was fickle into he bargain.

At the same time, she knew her concern was far less noble. She was just plain jealous, hating the way Krys gazed at Roger with such adoration—and the way he laughed down at her in return.

'Call me when you get back,' he had told Carrie. He hadn't made any promises, but she had assumed that meant he would be waiting for her.

'She who hesitates . . .' she told herself as she got ready for bed. There was little comfort in the thought. Nor in the fact that it was after midnight when Krys returned. Carrie had been awake most of the intervening hours, tormented by her thoughts.

Would Krys go back to his hotel with him? She was old enough, as she was fond of reminding Carrie. With a pang, Carrie realised how little she really knew her sister these days. She assumed that because Krys was so young, she was still a virgin. Yet nineteen was considered adult these days. Lots of girls were married with children by then.

The thought of Krys and Roger together at his hotel was exquisite torture, only alleviated when Carrie began stocktaking the book department in her head. The mental exercise was finally making her drowsy when she heard the scrape of a key in the front door. As her sister's footsteps slowed outside her bedroom door, Carrie pretended to be asleep until she heard Krys go into her own room.

There was no sign of Krys when Carrie emerged next
morning. She felt listless and heavy-eyed from lack of
sleep. Only a generous amount of eye make-up
disguised the violet shadows under her eyes.

The morning paper lay on the mat outside the door,
and Carrie picked it up, glancing at the headlines
unenthusiastically. Krys's door was still closed, so she
went into the kitchen to try to summon an appetite for
breakfast.

While the coffee was percolating, she leafed through
the paper, wondering what sort of voodoo made it fall
open at the comics page. Try as she might to
concentrate on the article on the opposite page, her eye
kept straying to 'The Many Loves of Emily'.

'Lucy, you're a witch,' she sighed aloud. Giving in,
she read the strip, panel by panel.

In the first panel, Lucy was helping Harvey down off
his ledge and into her apartment. 'You poor man,
you've caught a chill, and all because of me,' she
simpered.

'Wimp,' muttered Carrie.

Her irritation increased with the next panel in which
Lucy put the decorator to bed in her flat, plying him
with medicine and comfort. That he had caught the
chill because he was too dim-witted to know when he
wasn't wanted, everyone seemed to have forgotten.

She was toying with a bowl of muesli when Krys
appeared at the kitchen door, still in her dressing gown.
Her cheeks glowed and there was a diamond-bright
sparkle in her grey eyes.

'How was Mum?' she asked.

Before Carrie could say more than, 'Fine, she sent
you her love,' her sister threw herself on to a stool.
'Guess what?'

Curious in spite of herself, Carrie said, 'What?'

'I went to this amazing exhibition last night. The TV reporters were there. It was fabulous.'

'I know. I saw it on the news last night,' Carrie said guardedly.

She waited for Krys to say she had been with Roger, but Krys merely said, 'Fantastic! Did you see the size of the crowd?' Carrie nodded and Krys rolled her eyes expressively. 'What I wouldn't give for my work to draw a crowd the way a Gil Marten showing does! He's amazing. His eye for detail, and use of light and shade . . .'

'Whoa! I get the idea,' Carrie assured her, afraid that Krys was about to get technical. She was tempted to mention that she had also seen Roger on television, but she was afraid of what it could mean.

However, Krys had other things on her mind. 'I made my first sale last night,' she said breathlessly. 'One of the people Roger sent me to see was there and he wants to buy that big black and white lithograph of mine.' She named a price which made Carrie feel dizzy.

'That's more than I earn in a week!'

Krys's eyes shone. 'I know. Isn't it fabulous?'

Even while agreeing that it was fabulous, Carrie felt strangely bereft. In one short weekend, Krys had usurped not only her place with Roger, but her role as breadwinner as well. What had happened to her vulnerable little sister in such a short time? And where did it leave Carrie?

Somehow, she managed to finish her breakfast while Krys chattered on about the exhibition, oblivious of Carrie's mechanical responses. Only as she was leaving for work did Krys arrest her attention.

'By the way, did I mention that Roger's waiting for you to call him?'

Carrie froze in mid-stride. 'He is?'

'Yes. I ran into him at the showing and we talked for a while. He asked me to remind you to get in touch when you got home.'

Almost light-headed with relief, Carrie leaned against the door frame. 'The two of you weren't . . . together last night?'

'Good grief, no! He was the guest of honour. I was lucky he deigned to speak to me at all.' She frowned briefly. 'Poor man, he wasn't too well yesterday. He thinks he's coming down with something.'

Something hard and sharp pierced Carrie's lungs, restricting her breathing. 'He was ill last night?' Remembering the tanned, lithe man she had seen on the news the night before, it seemed impossible.

"Fraid so. He barely made it through the opening before he had to leave. Never mind, your call will cheer him up. He's not at the hotel, though. He thought a change of air might do him some good, so he's gone to this address.'

She gave Carrie a slip of paper bearing a Brooklyn address. The town was north of Sydney along the Hawkesbury River. She dropped the note into her handbag and recoiled in horror as she saw the time on her wristwatch. With a hasty goodbye to Krys, she fled down the stairs.

On the train to the city, she was too preoccupied to read. 'He wasn't with Krys, he wasn't with Krys, he wasn't with Krys,' the train wheels seemed to recite over and over again. She wanted to laugh aloud with relief, at the same time feeling ashamed of her suspicions. Why it was so important to her, she didn't want to examine too closely. All she knew was that suddenly she felt wonderful.

Only later did she remember this morning's Emily strip. Harvey had been taken ill then, too, and was being nursed back to health by Lucy. Was it yet another coincidence, or was Roger faking an illness so she would go running to his side?

Her mouth set in a firm line. Only hours before, she had been tortured by the idea of Roger going out with another woman—even if it was her own sister. Now, she was suspicious again. She wouldn't put it past him to have stage-managed the news report so she would get precisely the impression she did.

When would he learn that she was no Lucy?

She would indeed telephone him and express concern that he wasn't well. He could have all the 'there, theres' he wanted. But she was blowed if she was rushing off to some bush hideout to mop his fevered brow. If it really *was* fevered, she added mutinously to herself.

At lunch-time, she used up half her break trying to locate a public telephone from which she could make a long distance call, so she was feeling even more rebellious when she finally got through to him.

'Where on earth are you? You sound a million miles away,' she observed after hearing his voice, weak and faint, in response.

'I'm at Brooklyn with a temperature of a hundred and two and I feel like I'm dying,' came the hoarse reply.

Her heart felt as if someone was squeezing it tightly. 'You . . . you really *are* ill?'

'Didn't Krys tell you? I barely made it through last night's exhibition.'

'She told me,' Carrie said woodenly, not adding that

until she had heard his voice she didn't believe it. 'She didn't say what the matter was though.'

There was a long pause as if he was gathering his strength, then he said, 'I didn't know what it was myself. The doctor says it's a virus that's going around.'

Her sense of alarm was growing by the minute, and with it the certainty of what she must do next. 'Roger, is anyone there with you?' she asked.

She could picture him frowning in irritation. 'Sure, half a dozen blondes, why?'

He thought she was checking up on him! 'That wasn't what I asked,' she said briskly. 'I don't think you should be on your own in this condition.'

'You make me sound as if I'm bloody pregnant,' he growled. 'I don't need any nursemaids.'

At least his fighting spirit was intact, which was something. 'Well, I think you do,' she said firmly. 'Krys gave me the address where you're staying. It might take me a while to find it but I'll be there by this evening. Count on it.'

'Don't be ridiculous. I don't need . . .'

She cut across his objections. 'There's no point in arguing. I'm almost out of coins so I'll see you tonight.'

Almost as she said the words, the line went dead. She stared at the receiver in astonishment, as the full import of her promise struck her. She had just agreed to a two-hour drive to a small village along the Hawkesbury River to nurse Roger. There was no way she could get there by evening unless she left work early and she imagined Helen's reaction when she asked for the time off. They were up to their ears getting ready for stocktaking which started tomorrow. Yet she couldn't abandon Roger when he was obviously ill. He needed her. Somehow, she had to convince Helen that her errand was vital.

For once, the gods were with her. When she returned to the department still munching on the apple she'd snatched as a poor substitute for lunch, she was greeted by the young salesman from the computer department next door.

'The dragon lady tried to ring you in the canteen,' he said.

She ignored the nickname. 'I wasn't there. I had some errands to do. Why? What's the problem?'

He shrugged. 'Search me. She was called to a board meeting and it seems there were some books to be delivered to a school at Hornsby. They were promised for today and since your boss can't go, she asked me to tell you to do it.' He grinned. 'Lucky thing, you get the afternoon off.'

She could hardly believe her good fortune. Hornsby was on the way north. She shot a glance at her watch. If she worked like the very devil she could get her afternoon's work done, deliver the parcel to the school and have plenty of time for the drive to Brooklyn. How she would get back in time for work tomorrow was something she daren't even think about.

Determinedly, she stood up. She would do it. She had to—Roger needed her.

Only as she was tackling her afternoon's work did his words come back to haunt her. 'One day you won't be able to stop yourself kicking over the traces and doing something crazy . . .'

It was crazy, she had to agree. Leaving early to go to Roger's aid was the most impulsive thing she'd done in years. Yet it didn't feel crazy, as she drove north along the Pacific Highway, heading for the expressway which would cut miles off her journey. It felt good, as if the streak of daring had been there all along awaiting a means of expression.

She was on schedule, even after delivering the books to the school and calling at her flat to collect some clothes and leave a note for Krys. As soon as she knew that Roger was all right, she had decided to drive back again through the night, to be in time for work in the morning.

She made an effort to concentrate on the driving, watching carefully for the exit which would take her to the riverside town of Brooklyn.

Finding the turn-off was easy enough, but the road down to the village challenged her with its sharp bends and steep gradients. Locating the place where Roger was staying was even more of a challenge because many of the side streets lacked signposts and the light was rapidly failing. At last she pulled up outside a house which fitted Krys's directions. Looking at it, she drew a sharp breath of admiration. She had expected maybe a fisherman's cottage or a log cabin, anything but the long, low, hacienda-style house that hugged the hillside, its wide verandah looking out over a breath-taking view of the river.

She found her way along a brick-paved terrace to a main entrance where she pressed a bell and waited, wondering if she was in the right place.

'Carrie, is that you?' came a faint voice from inside as the last peals of the bell died away.

Instantly, she pushed open the door and went inside, finding herself in a wide, terrazzo-floored hallway with doors leading off it on both sides. On one side, she glimpsed a modern, country kitchen. She went to the other side and opened a door. 'Roger?'

He was lying on a wide Perspex couch with brown leather cushions and she dropped to her knees beside him. 'My God, what have you done to yourself?'

He looked terrible, the tanned skin turning sallow

while his lips were drawn tight over his teeth as if he was in pain. His hair was damp with perspiration and his eyes were cloudy. He focused on her with difficulty. 'I'll be all right. The doctor gave me something which made me groggy.'

Carrie stood up and stripped off her jacket, looking around for something to cover him. A Mexican-weave rug was draped over another couch and she placed it gently over him. 'Why didn't you tell me it was this bad?'

Roger passed a hand over his eyes. 'It wasn't when you called. It was only when that damned shot began to take effect ...'

'Maybe you're allergic to whatever was in it. I could call your doctor and check?'

He waved away her concern. 'No, he told me it would be like this, but he assured me it was only a twenty-four hour thing. I'll probably be fine in the morning.'

He didn't look as though he would be fine at all. 'Have you eaten anything?' she asked as the thought occurred to her.

'I had a scrambled egg this morning.'

'This morning? That was hours ago! I'll make you some soup or something.'

Before he could argue, she dropped her bag on the other couch and headed back to the kitchen she had glimpsed on her way in. It was splendidly equipped with dishwasher, waste-disposal unit and well-stocked cupboards and refrigerator. Whoever owned the place did well for himself.

From a cupboard she took some cans of chicken consommé and opened them, making toast while the soup simmered. The smell of the food aroused her own appetite, reminding her that an apple was the only thing between her and breakfast this morning.

While the soup was heating, the telephone rang. As soon as she confirmed that Roger Torkan was here but couldn't come to the phone, the caller launched into a tirade she was powerless to interrupt.

'Torkan thinks he can rearrange newspaper schedules to suit some purpose of his own—well, I went along, but only because Emily pulls readers . . . but the least he could do is get the replacement artwork in on time.'

'Are you Roger's editor?' she asked when she could get a word in edgewise.

There was a stunned pause. 'Who is this?'

'I'm a . . . a friend of Roger's. He was taken ill this morning and I came over to help out.'

'I see.' Another pause. 'I'm sorry. It seems I've made a fool of myself, sounding off at you. Call it deadline fever if you like. I really have to have the rest of this week's art.'

'You couldn't know he was ill,' she soothed the man. 'I'll tell Roger you were asking about the artwork. I'm sure he's made arrangements to get it to you.'

'I hope so,' the editor said wryly. 'Otherwise, I'll have a hole on Thursday's comics page.'

'I'll tell him,' she assured the editor again. When she gave Roger the message, he told her there was a packet of artwork on the hall table. 'I've booked a courier to collect it in the morning,' he explained wearily.

Before she could serve their dinner, the phone rang again and this time she was relieved to find Roger's doctor checking on his patient. She described Roger's alarming reaction to the shot, but the doctor confirmed that it was normal and she wasn't to worry. 'I'm glad he has someone with him, though,' the doctor said before he rang off.

But only for a few hours, Carrie thought worriedly. She daren't stay past midnight or, like Cinderella, her ball would be over. As she set the phone down, she noticed some unopened mail beside the telephone. It was addressed to Gil Marten. 'The wildlife artist,' she breathed, recalling the news programme last night. He must be a close friend of Roger's to allow him the free use of what was obviously an expensive property.

When she returned to the living-room with her laden tray, Roger was dozing but he roused sufficiently to eat a bowlful of the soup and some of the toast.

She eyed him with concern. 'Feeling better?'

He nodded. 'But not because of the soup.'

'Then what?'

His eyes, which had lost some of their alarming cloudiness, focused on her with a warmth which made her squirm. 'Can't you guess?'

Could her presence make such a difference? It was tempting to think so . . . but dangerous. It would mean she was important to him, when that was the last thing she wanted.

She didn't want him to be important to her either, not when he was everything she had learned to mistrust in a man.

The fact remained, though, that she had risked her job to come up here and look after him. She was too honest with herself to dismiss it as charity. She had simply been unable to stop herself. Roger needed her, which was all that mattered. Seeking a less disturbing train of thought, she said brightly, 'You must know Gil Marten very well.'

He frowned. 'I do, as it happens. Why do you ask?'

'I saw some of his mail in the kitchen. He has splendid taste if he decorated this place himself.'

'Gil Marten is a positive paragon,' Roger growled

back. 'He moves in all the right circles, paints respectable wildlife canvases, which raise thousands for worthy causes. In short, he's everything I'm not.'

'You don't sound as if you like him very much,' she observed. Could he be jealous of his friend's success?

Roger shrugged. 'He has his moments. I suppose you'd find him quite irresistible. After all, he's stable, respectable and wealthy.'

Uneasily, she looked away. She had evidently convinced Roger that they were the only things which mattered to her. 'I've no idea,' she said sharply, 'since I've never met the man. I don't think I've even seen a photo of him in the paper, come to think of it. He was supposed to have been at last night's art show wasn't he?'

His head jerked up. 'Yes, what of it?'

His aggressive tone made her uneasy but she put it down to his illness. 'N-nothing. I saw some of it on television, that's all. There was a close-up of you and Krys . . .'

He relaxed against the cushions. 'But none of my good friend, Gil. I see. Are you disappointed?'

'I told you, he means nothing to me. His property is lovely, I agree, but I don't covet it.' Suddenly she realised what he was driving at. 'Look, just because I want some security in my life doesn't make me some sort of gold-digger.'

As soon as she saw him close his eyes in pain, she regretted having spoken so sharply. 'I'm sorry,' she said quickly. 'Maybe we should discuss this some other time.'

He nodded and let her take the soup bowl from his hands so he could settle back. 'Cold?' she asked as she noticed how he hugged the rug around himself.

'A little.'

She bit her lip with anxiety. 'Shouldn't you go to bed where it's warmer?'

'I'm too bone weary to move,' he confessed, 'and you're too slight to carry me so don't even think about it.'

'I wasn't thinking anything so stupid. Where are the bedrooms and I'll get you some blankets?'

He gestured wearily towards the corridor. 'Second door on the left.'

She hurried out of the room and followed his directions, soon locating a master bedroom where she scooped up a fluffy continental quilt off the king-sized bed.

On the way back, she noticed another room opening off to the right. The door was ajar and beyond it was an artist's studio. This must be where Gil Marten worked. No wonder Roger resented the other man. He had nothing as luxurious as this in which to work.

But wasn't that his own fault? If he'd been more settled, as Gil Marten apparently was, he could have set himself up equally well. After all, he had some income from his book and his 'Emily' strip. There was no need for Roger to live in hotel rooms and borrowed houses, unless he squandered the money as quickly as he made it.

Roger's eyes were closed when she bent to drape the quilt over him, but he awoke at her touch. His hand snaked out and clasped her wrist, pulling her down on to the couch which was wide enough to accommodate two people.

'What are you doing?' she asked, startled.

'I need my love to keep me warm,' he murmured and shrugged the quilt over them both.

With his arm around her waist and his feverish body pressed against her, she couldn't summon the will to argue. It felt good being so close to him, aware of every muscle and contour of his powerful body outlined against her back and thighs.

Unable to resist, she bent her head and kissed the mouth which was only inches from hers. At once, her body throbbed with desire which she quelled with an effort of will.

He opened his eyes fractionally. 'Mmm, nice.' Then he closed them again and drifted off to sleep.

She couldn't move without disturbing him so she relaxed, only now realising how exhausted she was by the long drive and the previous night's restlessness.

His face was so close she could study every plane and angle in a way which would have discomfited her if he'd been awake. Her hand was pinned by his weight but she imagined her fingers tracing the firm jawbone, now shadowed with yellow stubble the way she'd first seen him.

He looked less formidable, more . . . she searched for a word . . . vulnerable. She wouldn't have thought it was possible, but the fierce, powerful Roger Torkan looked like a little boy when he was asleep.

His arm was heavy and hot across her body and she was warmed by his feverish heat. She felt cocooned and safe, held in the arms of the man she loved.

Her eyes had been closing steadily, drugged by the warmth, but now they flew open. Could it be? Surely she wasn't in love with Roger against all the dictates of her common sense?

Now she thought about it, all the evidence was there. How else could she explain the way he dominated her thoughts, or the peevish way she reacted to seeing him with Krys? Then there was her reckless flight up here, so out of character for her. It all added up. All the time that her head had been warning her against him, her heart had been following its own course.

What on earth was she to do? If he found out how she felt, he would pursue her even more keenly. He had made it clear he was attracted to her from the beginning. If he knew she loved him in return, he would never let her go. And he must! Life with Roger would be a repeat of what her mother had endured, which Carrie had vowed to avoid.

She hadn't bargained on a man like Roger coming along to batter down her carefully built defences. Her eyes roved over his face, so tranquil and boyish in sleep. He could be hers, she knew, and the idea tormented her.

She knew how it would be, having seen what marriage meant to Kay and Oscar. At its best, it would be wild, warm, funny and unpredictable. At its worst, it would be hell on earth until, finally, they destroyed each other.

Kay had been wise enough to divorce Oscar while they could still salvage something of their own lives. Would Carrie be able to give Roger up so easily? She doubted it. It was better not to start down that road in the first place.

The tragedy was, she was already half-way there and she didn't know whether there was any turning back.

CHAPTER SIX

SHE was awakened by the fierce rays of the morning sun shining into her eyes and she sat up in shock. So troubled had been her thoughts last night she hadn't expected to sleep at all. Now it was mid-morning. She should have been on her way back to the city hours ago.

The couch beside her was empty, and she absently caressed the hollow in the cushions where Roger had been then snatched her hand back hastily as she realised what she was doing. How could she have let him inveigle her into sleeping with him last night? She must have been more tired than she had allowed for.

Sleeping with him. The idea had all sorts of unwelcome associations, and she was relieved that none of them were true in the usual sense. He had been ill, needing the comfort of her nearness and her bodily warmth; there was nothing more to it.

At least, that was his excuse. What was hers? She had none, she knew. After he drifted off to sleep, she could have slipped out of his embrace. Instead she had chosen to stay, and the memory of his lithe body pressed against hers sent shudders of longing through her.

Determinedly, she swung her legs to the floor. The clatter of dishes told her Roger was in the kitchen so she tiptoed past the closed door and went to a bathroom she'd glimpsed last night.

While she had a quick shower, she hung her crumpled skirt and blouse over the shower rail to let the steam iron out the worst of the wrinkles. She looked much more presentable by the time she was dressed again, with her hair neatly brushed.

Roger was pouring freshly brewed coffee into cups when she joined him in the kitchen. He looked up and smiled. 'I thought I heard you pottering about. Sleep well?'

'I wasn't supposed to sleep at all. Helen will kill me when I roll up late!'

'Then why roll up at all?' he suggested teasingly. 'Why not call in sick or something?'

She ignored the tempting thought. 'Speaking of sick people, you look uncommonly well this morning.'

'Try not to sound so disappointed! I told you it was a twenty-four-hour thing. Actually, looks can be deceiving. I feel dog-tired, as if someone was using my body for a punching bag, but whatever the doc gave me cured the rest of the symptoms so I can't complain.' He handed her a cup of coffee. 'Breakfast?'

Still astonished by his recuperative powers, she shook her head. 'I'll drink this and be on my way.'

'Do you really have to go?'

She hesitated. 'I'm not exactly enthusiastic about it.'

'Then don't go. Stay here. I need you. Why, I might have a relapse at any moment.'

She almost choked on her coffee. 'You look more like you could run the four-minute mile—in three minutes!'

He regarded her seriously. 'Then stay because you want to, and because I want you to.'

When he looked at her with those beguiling blue eyes she could feel her resistance melting away. 'All right,' she breathed. 'The store does owe me some time off—although what Helen will think when I ask for it during stocktaking, I hate to imagine!'

'Can't you tell her it's an emergency, that you're nursing a sick friend?'

'But what if she asks who the sick friend is?'

He grinned. 'You'll have to tell her, won't you?'

'I can't,' she said unhappily. 'If someone from the switchboard overheard me, it would be all over Petrie's in hours. I'll have to think of something else.'

'Then say you aren't feeling well yourself. You can't be feeling too good after such a disturbed sleep.'

Now that he mentioned it, she did fell heavy with fatigue. The lack of sleep the previous night, coupled with a long drive here and another difficult night had taken their toll. 'Very well,' she agreed, 'but it's your fault for corrupting me, remember?'

He caressed the back of her neck, lifting the tiny hairs so she shivered with pleasure. 'I have not yet begun to corrupt you,' he warned her.

As she expected, Helen was annoyed when Carrie requested the time off owing to her.

'You might have given me some warning,' she grumbled. 'I'll be lucky to get a casual in to replace you at such short notice.'

'I'm sorry. I didn't know I was going to feel like this this morning,' Carrie explained. It was the truth as far as it went.

At once, Helen relented. 'Why didn't you say you were ill? Of course you can't come in if you aren't feeling well. Is there anything I can do for you?'

It was hard enough keeping her voice level while she stretched the truth but Carrie found it nearly impossible not to giggle and ruin her credibility, when Roger started stroking the back of her neck and dropping teasing kisses along her hairline.

'N-no thanks, Helen,' she said with an effort. 'I'll be fine. All I need is a rest.'

'Would you like me to call your doctor?' Helen asked. 'You sound as if you're having difficulty breathing.'

Carrie ducked Roger's outstretched hand. 'I'll be all right, really, but I feel terrible about the stocktaking.'

'Don't give it another thought. It isn't the end of the world if it isn't finished today. You take it easy and hopefully you'll be well enough to come in tomorrow.'

'Thanks, Helen, see you.'

As she hung up, Carrie whirled on Roger, her face scarlet with guilt. 'I wish she hadn't been so kind. Now I feel terrible.'

He looked chastened, although she was sure he couldn't feel worse than she did. 'It's not as if you told her any lies.'

'But I didn't correct her when she got the idea that I was ill, so it was lying by omission. I feel like such a heel.'

Roger enfolded her in his arms and drew her close against him. He was still in his woollen dressing-gown and the coarse fabric teased her through her silk blouse. 'Is that how you feel when you're with me?'

In spite of herself, she laughed, her body automatically quickening in response to his nearness. 'Of course not.'

He looked down at her fondly. 'I believe this is the first time in your life that you ever did anything crazy. Do you always play so strictly by the rules?'

Remembering a father who never had, she sobered. 'Mostly, although I didn't yesterday.'

'No, you didn't, did you? What made you come flying up here to play Florence Nightingale?'

Looking down, she pressed both palms against his chest as if symbolically to put some distance between them. 'I don't know. I suppose I was worried about you. Any friend would have done what I did.'

He put a hand under her chin and eased her head up until she was forced to meet those startling blue eyes.

'Any friend wouldn't have shared the couch with me all night.'

'I . . . I didn't mean to. You were cold. It was the easiest way to warm you,' she lied desperately. 'I must have dozed off.'

He laughed huskily, the sound sending goosebumps up and down her spine. 'I know. I woke up in the middle of the night to find you in my arms. One arm had gone totally numb underneath you.'

'You should have woken me.'

He shook his head. 'No way. You might have insisted on sleeping elsewhere, and I found I enjoyed holding you so close. I was tempted to wake you once, though.'

'What for?' she asked, then could have bitten her tongue off as she saw the challenging gleam in his eye. 'Oh, you!'

'Well, we've slept together but we haven't really . . . slept together,' he said, his tone caressing. 'Waking up to find you in my arms gave me all sorts of ideas.'

She didn't know whether to be glad or sorry that he had let her sleep. Impatient with herself, she twisted free and turned towards the stove. 'Since I'm staying for a while, why don't you get dressed while I make breakfast?'

He dropped a kiss on to the top of her head. 'Practical as always,' he sighed. 'Have it your way. The courier's already been so you don't have to worry about my artwork. And you can use anything you find in the cupboards or the fridge.'

'Mr Marten is a generous host,' she observed.

He puckered his brow. 'What? Oh, sure.' He crossed two fingers and held them up. 'Gil and I are like that.'

Yet last night Roger acted as if he was jealous of his

friend's success, she thought as she pottered around the kitchen.

'One day, I'd like to meet your Gil Marten,' she told Roger over breakfast.

He glowered at her over the scrambled eggs. 'I'm not that big a fool.'

'What do you mean?'

'Knowing that he's everything you ever dreamed of in a man, do you think I'd be silly enough to introduce him to you?'

She busied herself buttering her toast. Roger must believe she was utterly materialistic if he was afraid to introduce her to his well-to-do friend. 'Do you think I'm going to swoon all over him because he has money?' she asked crossly.

'You can't really blame me for thinking so,' he observed moodily. 'You've made it clear how much you value security.'

'Security isn't necessarily money,' she sighed. 'Oh, Roger, please don't let's argue. I don't often have a day like this to myself.'

Imploringly, she reached out a hand to him. He turned her wrist so he was holding her hand. 'Very well. I won't say any more for the moment. We'll try and make this a day to remember, shall we?'

He was as good as his word. Although she worried that he might still be too weak, he insisted on taking her out on the river in a small aluminium boat that was kept moored to a jetty at the back of the house.

After showing her how to fish with a cork handline, he shared her excitement when she caught a small bream. They added several more to the bag, and by lunch-time they had enough for a meal. While she made a salad in the kitchen, he barbecued the fish on the

terrace. Then they sat in the sunshine, eating the golden
fish with their fingers.

'This is wonderful,' she said, unaware that her
shining eyes and sun-kissed skin had brought a gleam
of excitement to his eyes.

He gazed at her with disturbing directness. 'That's
because you are.'

'Roger, don't . . .'

'Don't what? Tell you how I feel? I've been wanting
to for days now. In a way, I'm almost glad I was ill so I
could have this chance to talk to you, alone.'

Her bent head shielded her confusion from him. She
had sensed this was coming and she still didn't know
how she should answer him. She was torn between her
heart, which longed to tell him of the love she had
discovered for him only last night, and her head, which
warned her of the consequences if she did. 'What would
you like to talk about?' she asked softly.

'Me. You. I want to know everything about you.
What is your mother like, for instance?'

She could almost hear his thoughts. Like mother, like
daughter. She was afraid he was in for a disappointment. 'She's nothing like me,' she confessed. 'Kay is
willowy and blonde, like a smaller, finer version of
Krys.'

'Then you must take after your father,' he said,
referring to her elfin dark looks.

She did but she wasn't proud of it. 'Only in
appearance.'

He picked up her bitterness immediately. 'He must
have some good qualities, or your mother wouldn't
have married him—and given him two such exquisite
daughters.'

The compliment made her colour but she bit her lip
as she wondered how to answer. She sensed that Roger

wouldn't settle for less than the truth. 'Oscar is a good man, I suppose,' she said with difficulty. 'He can be very entertaining to have around.'

When she and Krys were children, Oscar used to amuse them with lightning sketches to illustrate the old fairy tales. She shrugged the memory away. 'Why should you want to talk about him? It's not as if you ever met him.' Or are likely to, she added to herself.

Roger stared off into the distance. 'Oh, but I have— at least, I believe it was him. Oscar Doyle was responsible for me becoming a cartoonist.'

Carrie stared at him. Oh no! Fate couldn't be so cruel! Surely Oscar couldn't have had this far-reaching an effect on her life.

But it seemed that he had!

'I was about fifteen, just starting to plan my life,' Roger reminisced. 'I never wanted to be anything except an artist, but my father was against it. He wanted me to study law, which I hated. If he found art materials in my room, he destroyed them. I got into the habit of sketching with the most basic materials, sometimes only paper and pencil.'

'Was that how you started cartooning?'

He nodded. 'It was the best medium for the materials I had access to. I used to go off into the bush by myself all weekend, drawing everything I saw in caricature. I didn't think I could make a career of it when Dad was so antagonistic, but I wanted to go on drawing for as long as I could before I had to give it up.'

'But you never did give it up. What happened?'

He regarded her tenderly, brushing a strand of hair away from her eyes. 'Out in the bush, I met another artist. We worked side by side for a while, then we had lunch together. I told him how I felt about art. He wanted to know why I wasn't studying seriously. I told him about my father and I got the impression he understood exactly what I was up against.'

Watching Roger, Carrie felt a lump rise in her throat. If it had been Oscar, his experience with his own family would have told him just how Roger felt. 'Did he tell you his name?'

'No, but his drawing style was very distinctive. I went to the National Gallery in Canberra to see if I could spot it again. I'm pretty sure it was him.'

Roger was showing her a side of her father she had never seen, and it was so at odds with the self-centred image she held that she wanted to reject it outright. 'Whatever he said must have had a tremendous effect if you've remembered that meeting all this time.'

'It changed my life. He made me see that if I wanted something badly enough I should go after it and not let anything stand in my way. He gave me the courage to stand up to my father. To my surprise, he accepted it. He never helped me much but he didn't oppose me after that either.'

Idly, she drew patterns on the quarry tiles with her bare foot. 'It's quite a story.'

'Now it's your turn. Tell me about your childhood.'

She debated how much to tell him, but most of it was too painful so she shied away from even talking about it. 'Some of it you already know,' she said at last. 'Oscar left us when I was fourteen—a few years before you met him, I'd say. My mother had a struggle to keep things going, then a distant relative left her Megalong.' At his questioning look, she elaborated. 'It's one of those run-down mansions in the Blue Mountains. We all pitched in to make it presentable, then Mum was able to let the rooms and make a living.'

His expression was admiring. 'She sounds like a resourceful woman, your mother.'

She compressed her lips. 'She didn't have much choice.'

'Can't you forgive Oscar even now?'

With her free hand, she ruffled her hair restively. 'What for? For bringing children into the world then leaving them high and dry?'

He stood up, towering over her so she was in his shadow. 'Well, I'm grateful to him, anyway.'

'For supporting your choice of career?'

His face was alarmingly close as he bent nearer. 'No, for giving me the girl of my dreams.' As she opened her mouth to argue, he pressed a finger against her lips. 'Hush—I mean it. I've known you were the one for me since the day we met. I love you, Carrie, and I want to marry you.'

'You—you can't know what you're saying. It's been too short a time.'

His eyes half closed and his lips parted into a sensuous smile, which hinted at his inner thoughts. 'Time doesn't matter in our case. There's a chemistry between us which tells me you're the woman for me. Surely nothing else matters?'

Panic-stricken, she half twisted away from him. 'No, it isn't all that matters. You . . . you can't live on love.'

Abruptly, he straightened, the warmth draining from his face as he looked at her with contempt. 'You'd trade in what we could have for a regular pay packet and a suburban bungalow? I can't believe you mean it.'

Tears of frustration gathered behind her eyelids but were held in check by her anger. 'Is that so wrong? I saw what my mother went through for love—what she's still going through for that matter. Even now, she may have to sell her home if costs get any higher.'

Compassion warred with frustration in his face.

'Maybe I could help. Just give me a chance instead of making me fight phantoms.'

How could he help? Living in borrowed homes and hotel rooms, from commission to commission. 'It's no use, it wouldn't work.'

He turned his back, tormenting her with the sight of those muscles which had rippled under her hands only last night, and the strong fingers which had caressed her so pleasurably. She mustn't think of such things, only of the futility of a continuing relationship with him.

If only she could make him understand. She wasn't rejecting him, only his way of life. She stretched out her hand to him. 'Roger, please . . .'

They were interrupted by a commotion in the driveway as a plum-coloured Porsche screeched to a stop below the terrace, scattering the bush birds which were feeding off the crumbs of lunch.

'Coo-ee!' trilled a feminine voice as Bianca West stepped out of the car. 'Is it a private party or can anyone join?'

With a furious glance at her, Roger leaned against the railing and waved to Bianca. 'Come on up. We could use some good humour up here.'

His strategy was obvious. Having been rebuffed by Carrie, he was going to use Bianca to get even. Well let him! It only proved how right Carrie had been to turn him down.

Bianca pretended surprise to find Carrie on the terrace. 'Slave's day off?' she asked archly.

Before Carrie could answer, Roger handed the newcomer a tall, iced drink. 'How did you find me—Miss West, wasn't it?'

'Bianca, please. Your agent told me about this place. He wasn't keen at first, but when I told him I was interested in buying some of your work . . .'

The muscles in Roger's jaw worked. 'He would.'

The woman grazed a hand over Roger's forearm and Carrie noted that he didn't object. 'Your agent also said you were ill. All better now?'

'Fully recovered. It was one of those bugs which knock you around for a while, then they go as quickly as they come.' He looked over his shoulder at Carrie. 'Luckily I had good medical care.'

Not to mention personal attention, she thought miserably. He wasn't going to tell Bianca about that, though, in case it spoiled his chances with her. You can't have your cake and eat it, she told herself crossly, but was well aware that she wanted to.

She knew exactly what Roger was up to. He thought if he played up to Bianca it would show Carrie what she was missing. Instead, it confirmed that she had made the only decision she could.

She stood up. 'I'd better be getting back to town. I don't want to interrupt your business discussion.'

He started to follow her but Carrie was already half-way through the front door. 'Don't bother about me. I'll get my things and be on my way. You see to your guest.'

She could imagine what language he would like to use, but he only let his breath out in an explosive gust. 'I'll do that, and to hell with you!' He turned on his heel.

Alone in the dim cool of the house, she was tempted to throw herself down on one of the couches and howl, but she had made her bed so now she must lie on it— alone. She gathered her bag and jacket and went down to her car, throwing a cursory goodbye over her shoulder.

His cartoon character, Lucy, couldn't have carried an exit off with more aplomb, she thought as she drove away. At the same time, she recognised the thought as bravado. Leaving Roger with Bianca had been an act of self-preservation, not of choice.

When Roger proposed marriage to her she had been sorely tempted to say yes. He was right about the powerful attraction that existed between them—she had been aware of it from the moment she set eyes on him at the store. But she dared not give in to it. With a father like Oscar, it would be the height of foolishness.

All the same, as she hurtled down the expressway towards Sydney, she couldn't help wondering which decision made her more of a fool.

Krys wasn't at home when she got there and she wandered around the empty flat, finally picking up the morning paper which Krys had left on the breakfast bar. She turned to the comics page, making a bet with herself that Harvey had also proposed to Lucy. Would she turn him down if so?

In the first panel, Harvey was indeed on his knees in front of Lucy. Still convalescing in her apartment, he was in his dressing-gown and looked very funny in the classic proposal scene. Lucy, whose likeness to Carrie still disturbed her, had her head turned away. Her speech bubble said, 'Free wallpaper for life just isn't enough, Harvey.'

Carrie's smile froze on her lips. Roger made her sound like an opportunist who put material things ahead of all else, even love.

'This is stupid—Lucy isn't me,' she reminded herself. But wasn't there a similarity? Like Lucy, Carrie had turned down Roger's proposal because he couldn't offer her a secure future. He had even anticipated her reasons when he drew today's strip.

Why couldn't he understand that it was emotional security she craved, not money? She wanted a husband who knew she was alive—unlike Oscar who could, and did, ignore his family's existence when he was immersed in a project. She wanted a man who put her needs first.

She sniffed noisily. Why couldn't Roger just take no for an answer, instead of taunting her with his wretched cartoon characters?

Angrily, she screwed up the newspaper and flung it away, then smoothed it out and replaced it on the breakfast bar. 'Damn you, Roger!' she seethed, unwilling to concede that the cartoon affected her so strongly because it hit so close to home.

A moment later, she reached a decision. It was late in the day but she would go to the store and confess to Helen that she wasn't really ill. The way she felt about Roger was bad enough, without having her conscience bothering her as well.

Her good intentions were to no avail, however, because Helen was out when Carrie arrived at the store. Michael from the next department informed her that her boss wouldn't be back until almost closing time.

'It's just as well you weren't here this morning,' he told her with some relish. 'She was in a real stew about something.'

'It wasn't because of my absence?' Carrie asked.

'It wouldn't have helped. But she didn't blow up until she got a phone call an hour ago.'

A supplier must have let her down or something, Carrie mused, then decided that worrying wouldn't help whatever the problem was. She rolled up her sleeves and set to work to help the casuals stocktake the piles of books.

A few copies of Roger's book remained and her hand lingered on them, her finger tracing the outline of his photo on the back cover. What would it be like to be his wife, to share his bed and be the object of his passion? she wondered, then chased the thoughts away. She had made the only decision she could if she was to have any sort of decent life.

With a determined gesture, she thrust the books back on to the shelf. She'd better not let Helen find her mooning over Roger's photo when she returned. It wouldn't help her case one bit.

As it turned out, Helen wouldn't have been surprised. As soon as she strode in, she called Carrie into her office, motioning her to close the door behind her.

'I see you have recovered from your sudden illness,' she said tartly.

Carrie lowered her lashes. 'I wanted to speak to you about that.'

'Actually, so did I. But you first.'

She took a deep breath. 'I . . . I wasn't really ill when I phoned this morning.'

Helen's eyebrow arched. 'Really? Do tell me more.'

She wasn't making this easy, Carrie thought, then acknowledged that her behaviour didn't warrant any better treatment. She found herself pouring out the story of Roger's illness, her flight to his side and the tiredness that had prompted her to ask for time off this morning. 'I'm sorry I let you believe I was ill,' she said at last.

Helen's face was impassive. 'I'm glad you decided to be honest with me,' she said. 'You see, I had a call from Bianca West just before I went out.'

Carrie drew a strangled breath. She should have known that Bianca would do something like reporting her to her boss. No wonder Helen left in such a temper. Dishonesty was the one failing she simply couldn't abide. She waited for the storm to break.

To her amazement, Helen leaned forward, her expression softening. 'Don't look so terrified, child. Don't you think I know how it feels to be in love?'

As Carrie stared at her boss, Helen gestured impatiently. 'I know what sort of reputation I have. "Dragon lady" is one of the kinder descriptions, I believe. But I was your age once and I know how strong those feelings can be.' Carrie nodded dumbly and Helen went on more briskly, 'However, I must say I am very disappointed in you, Caroline. I had high hopes for you taking over this department one day.'

With a shock, Carrie realised Helen was using the past tense. 'Am I fired?' she asked hoarsely.

'Of course not. You're capable of good work and I believe you have a future in retailing, but not as my assistant, I'm afraid. You know how I feel about honesty—I can only work with someone in whom I have full confidence. But rather than lose your talents altogether, I'm recommending you for transfer to another department.'

Carrie's heart sank. Being in the book department was the only thing which made working in the store bearable. 'B-but, I don't want to work anywhere else,' she gasped.

'You should have considered that before you misled me,' Helen said, but more kindly.

There was only one thing left for her to do. 'Then I'm afraid I shall have to resign,' she whispered, her voice breaking.

'Aren't you being childish? You have a good future in this business if you apply yourself.' Her expression softened momentarily. 'I'm sorry this had to happen, Caroline. I wish I could keep you on here. Perhaps after you've had some wider experience in the store ...'

The implication was that she could return to the book department after she had served out her punishment, but she shook her head. 'It wouldn't work, Helen. I know you're trying to be fair, but maybe this is for the best.' Already an idea was forming in her mind. 'Maybe I needed something like this to jolt me out of my rut.'

Helen regarded her as if she'd gone mad. 'Whatever are you talking about?'

Feeling suddenly light-hearted, Carrie stood up. 'Nothing at all, Helen. Thanks for everything.'

She could feel Helen watching her curiously as she returned to the department to get her handbag. There was still time to visit the personnel department and put her resignation into effect, before she changed her mind.

To her relief, the personnel manager agreed to her request not to serve out her notice, and arranged for her to be paid off on the spot.

Carrie walked out of the store with her accumulated holiday pay and salary in her wallet, wondering what had come over her.

'You did what?' Krys asked at home later, when Carrie told her what she'd just done.

Carrie explained about giving in her notice rather than be moved to another department. She didn't mention the idea that was growing in her mind, preferring to investigate it fully first. She also left out any mention of Roger's part in her decison.

All the same, Krys said shrewdly, 'Your spending the night with Roger didn't have anything to do with this, I suppose?'

Carrie felt her colour rising. 'I didn't spend the night with him, at least not in the way you mean. He was ill and I looked after him, that was all.'

Krys looked sceptical. 'Whatever you say, big sister. What are you going to do now, with no job?'

It was a real role reversal, Carrie thought, remembering Krys's announcement not so long ago. She forced herself to smile reassuringly. 'Don't worry, Krys. I'll think of something. I always have before.'

To her surprise, Krys grinned broadly. 'This time, you don't have to, big sister. Your news sidetracked me a little, but I have some of my own. I've been invited to show my work at the Glenfield Gallery.'

Carrie stared at her, astonished. 'Do you have enough work for an exhibition?'

'Not on my own. The gallery is doing a pop art exhibition. I'm only one of the participants. The featured artist is Gil Marten. Oh, Carrie, to think my work will be hanging alongside his!'

'But surely you won't be paid until your work is sold?'

'That's the good part. Glenfield give you an advance on sales—just like in book publishing. I'll be able to take care of our expenses until you get organised. It's the least I can do after all you've done for me.'

Carrie felt suddenly deflated. The sense of purpose that had sustained her all day deserted her in a rush. She must be crazy, resigning her job to follow a foolish dream. Hadn't she condemned her father, and then Krys, for doing the same thing? She was glad she hadn't confided her plans to Krys straight away. Morning might well find her back at Petrie's asking for her job back.

Krys was watching her carefully. 'You don't seem very pleased with my news,' she said in a small voice.

Impulsively, Carrie hugged her sister. 'Of course I am.' It was just that she needed time to get used to the change in their relationship, she added, but kept this thought to herself.

Giving up Roger had been hard enough. Now she couldn't even take comfort from her accustomed 'big sister' role.

'There's something else,' Krys said diffidently. 'I'm

not sure how to tell you.'

A prickle of apprehension crept up Carrie's neck but she smiled encouragingly. 'Sometimes just blurting it out is best.'

'The gallery thought it would be a novel idea to exhibit some of Dad's work as well.'

Relief made Carrie smile. 'Is that all?'

'Then you're pleased?'

'Of course.' Oddly enough, she was. Maybe it was her sister's infectious enthusiasm but under the circumstances she couldn't even resent Oscar intruding on their lives yet again.

Krys breathed a sigh of relief. 'I'm so glad! It makes it easier to ask you . . .'

'Ask me what?'

'Since you won't be working for a while, would you help me organise my share of the exhibition?'

'Of course I will. I'd be delighted. What would I have to do?'

Krys turned aside, studying her fingernails with great concentration. 'Oh . . . send out some press releases, help me get my work ready for showing and . . .' She paused.

'And?' Carrie prompted.

'Go and see Dad and collect the works he's putting into the exhibition. I was wondering how on earth to manage it. You being available is like the answer to a prayer. Please, Carrie, say you'll do it?'

Go and see the father she had banished from her life when he left? With a sense of unreality, she heard herself saying, 'Of course; I'll be glad to help in any way I can.'

CHAPTER SEVEN

A few days later, Carrie was so nervous at the prospect of seeing her father again that she regretted ever saying she would be the one to go.

'Relax, it's only Dad,' said Krys unhelpfully, watching Carrie pace the floor again.

'It's different for you. You've kept in touch with him. I haven't seen him since I was fourteen.'

Krys looked at her with compassion. 'Do you think it will make any difference? Whatever you think of him, he's still our father. He loves you, you know.'

All the same, Carrie felt tied up in knots inside, torn between wondering what Oscar would be like, and wishing she didn't have to find out. When Krys offered to recruit one of her friends to share the driving, she agreed with alacrity. Anything was better than confronting her father alone.

'Who will you ask? One of your girlfriends from university?' she asked, hardly caring.

'Oh, I'll think of someone,' Krys said diffidently.

If Carrie hadn't been so preoccupied with her anxiety over seeing her father again, she might have questioned Krys more closely. As it was, she was so thankful to have an ally on the expedition that it never occurred to her to ask who Krys had found until the day of the trip itself.

'It's a surprise,' Krys said firmly. 'He's waiting outside in the car for you.'

Carrie raised an eyebrow, curious at long last. 'He? Do you think that's a good idea?'

'In this case, definitely.' Krys handed Carrie her overnight bag and pressed her arm reassuringly. 'Give Dad my love, won't you?'

A mist filmed Carrie's eyes and she blinked furiously. 'Of course.'

'And make sure he picks the best of his sketches for the exhibition,' Krys added as she saw her sister to the door.

Carrie's car was already packed and ready for the trip, since Krys had said her friend didn't own a car. He *must* be one of Krys's friends from university, she decided as she went downstairs. The idea of undertaking an overnight trip in completely strange company suddenly seemed foolhardy. How could she have let Krys talk her into it without checking her companion out more closely?

Well, it was too late now. She would have to trust Krys's judgement, nerve-wracking though it seemed. Quickening her steps, she hurried out to the car-ports at the back of the apartment building.

When she saw who was waiting in the car, her steps faltered and she felt herself go pale. 'Roger! What are you doing here?'

'I'm your escort for the trip to Kempsey. Didn't Krys tell you?'

'She . . . she said one of her friends would share the driving but . . .'

'She didn't tell you which friend, and you were in such a stew about seeing your father again that you didn't press her for details,' he finished for her.

Carrie let her overnight case drop to the concrete. 'We can't travel together. I'd rather manage by myself.'

'It's a five-hour drive and I understand Oscar lives in pretty rugged bushland. Are you sure you want to go alone?'

Put like that, it did sound daunting but she set her mouth resolutely. 'All the same, you know why we can't go together.'

His eyes became hooded. 'Is it me you don't trust—or yourself?'

Heat surged through her limbs. 'Oh, I trust you,' she said hastily.

'Then it must be your own behaviour you're worried about!'

He was impossible! She couldn't make more of an issue of it without confirming his guess. Picking up her case, she strode around to the driver's side and got in, tossing the case into the back seat. 'Do I have your word that you won't try to ... to seduce me on this trip?'

He grinned, making her want to slap him. 'You have my word I won't do anything you don't want me to,' he said solemnly.

It was something at least. She gunned the motor to life. 'I still think this is crazy but I don't seem to have much choice. I'll drive the first couple of hundred kilometres, then you take over. OK?'

He settled himself more comfortably and snapped the seat belt across his expansive chest. 'Anything you say, sweetheart.'

His apparent compliance didn't fool her one bit. It was bad enough that she was on tenterhooks about the reunion with Oscar—now she had Roger's disturbing nearness to contend with as well.

He was right—she didn't trust herself with him. Knowing how she felt about him, it would be all too easy to let him make love to her. In a moment of abandon, she might even agree to marry him against all common sense. Was that what he was hoping would happen when he agreed to come on this trip? She was glad she had his word to let her make the running. She would just have to make sure things were very circumspect between them throughout the trip.

'Still mad at me?' he asked, interrupting her thoughts.

'Why should I be?'

'You left Brooklyn fast enough when Bianca West rolled up.'

She kept her eyes on the road. 'It was none of my business.'

'Then you don't want to know what happened after you left?'

Her fingers tightened around the steering wheel. 'No, I don't.'

'Pity, because nothing did.'

Before she could prevent it, she gave a snort of derision, realising that she had betrayed her interest immediately.

'You do care,' he said at once.

'N-no, you're wrong,' she denied but without conviction. In truth, she was relieved to find there was nothing between Roger and Bianca West. It shouldn't have mattered to her. She had turned him down. But it did matter and she couldn't deny it to herself.

'Did she buy any of your drawings?' she asked, trying to deflect the conversation on to a less personal note.

There was amusement in his tone as he answered, 'She bought some of Gil Marten's work instead.'

Carrie shot him a look of sympathy. 'Oh, Roger, I'm sorry. She wasted your time and didn't even buy any of your stuff.'

'That's all right. I told you Gil's work is more respectable, and more valuable if you're buying for investment, as I gather Bianca was.'

Her breath whistled out between clenched teeth.

Why wasn't he as cross as she was about Bianca's actions? He was as bad as her father—no head for business. 'Couldn't you have persuaded her to invest in some of your drawings?' she asked tightly.

He grinned. 'You mean use my charms on her? From the come-on she was giving me, she would have enjoyed the attempt. But I don't believe in hard sell.'

He was hopeless! 'Now I see why Gil Marten is so successful and you aren't!' she said in frustration.

There was a long silence and she began to regret her outburst. She didn't want to hurt Roger, only to see him succeed for his sake.

She remembered reading a poem about travelling to the beat of a different drummer. Roger was like that, viewing success in different terms from herself. He really *was* like her father. This time, she was surprised to find herself grudgingly admiring him rather than condemning him for it.

She reached across and touched his arm lightly, then returned her hand to the wheel. 'I'm sorry,' she said softly. 'For comparing you to Gil Marten, I mean. It was unfair of me.'

'Don't worry, I'm used to it,' he said, and his voice held a puzzling irony. 'The guy haunts me wherever I go.'

It was out before she could stop it. 'Then why hang around him so much? Why not cut yourself free of his influence?'

'I can't,' he said awkwardly. 'We're ... sort of ... related.'

Now she had it. The successful member of the family looking after the black sheep. 'Is he a cousin or what?'

'Or what,' he answered flatly. Obviously he didn't intend to enlighten her.

Remembering how jealous Roger had been when she

asked for an introduction, she said, 'I see.'

He gazed intently out of the window. 'Do you?' Then he twisted back to her. 'Let's not talk about him. Let's talk about us.'

'There isn't any "us",' she reminded him.

'There is now. I understand you lost your job because of me—so you have no choice but to marry me.'

She screwed up her face at him. 'It wasn't because of you, at least not directly.'

'But Krys told me Helen was so upset over you letting her think you were ill, that you had to resign—which makes it my fault.'

'For goodness' sake, don't be such a . . . a Harvey,' she snapped back. 'Krys doesn't know the whole story.'

'But you're going to tell me?'

He had her in a corner. If she didn't tell him, he would probably nag her the whole five hundred kilometres. 'All right,' she sighed, 'Helen didn't fire me. She was very upset about the deception, and wanted me to transfer to another department. I decided now was as good a time as any to put into action a plan I've had in mind for some time.' Since she met Roger, to be precise, but she avoided adding that.

'Go on. What plan?'

'I've decided to find myself a part-time job so I can go back to school during the day to qualify as a teacher.'

He straightened. 'Carrie, that's wonderful! Good for you!'

'So you see, inadvertently, you acted as a catalyst when you suggested I take that day off. If I hadn't got into trouble with Helen, I might still be in my cosy rut.'

'Didn't I say you possessed a spirit of adventure which was waiting to get out?'

She sighed. 'Do you always have to be right?'

He laughed. 'I was right about you, anyway. You're

like a chrysalis, Carrie, turning into a butterfly before my eyes. I only hope my net is strong enough to hold you when you fully emerge.'

Trust an artist to be so fanciful! 'There isn't a strong enough net in the world for that,' she said, laughing in spite of herself. 'I still prefer to rely on my own resources. It's less of a let-down.'

The atmosphere between them chilled suddenly. 'You're determined to believe I would let you down, aren't you.' It wasn't a question. His tone supplied the answer for them both.

She squirmed uncomfortably in the driver's seat, glad to have the driving to occupy her. Couldn't he see that it was one thing to change your whole outlook on life? Just because she had been adventurous enough to try to follow her dream of teaching, didn't mean she was ready for a lifetime of insecurity such as Kay had endured.

A frosty silence settled over the car, and there was no more small talk as they headed north along the Pacific Highway. They left the highway at Buladelah and followed the Lakes Way through several coastal fishing towns before stopping for a lunch of fried chicken, eaten by the roadside at Taree.

After lunch Roger took the wheel and they drove along the coastline until they reached the Oxley Highway junction. At Kempsey, they turned towards Bellbrook, following Krys's directions to the artists' colony where Oscar lived.

Since their last altercation, conversation had been limited to observations about the scenery and the weather. Now they needed all their concentration to follow the side roads that wound upwards to the Carrai Plateau, high above the Macleay River Valley.

'It's absolutely beautiful!' Carrie breathed, her finger

poised over a road map.

'It's breathtaking country up here,' Roger agreed, sounding civil for the first time in hours. 'I roamed around here a lot as a boy. I guess this is where I acquired my taste for prehistoric jungle.'

Prehistoric it certainly appeared. The dense undergrowth was festooned with giant strangler figs, elkhorns, staghorns and flowering orchids. Bellbirds, lyre birds and fluorescent-hued parrots brought the forest to life, while on the ground they saw kangaroos, wallabies and an occasional scrub turkey.

It was mid-afternoon by the time they came to a rustic post-and-rail fence with a hand-lettered sign swinging from it. 'Koompartoo—wildlife reserve, no shooters,' Carrie read.

'Hmm, "fresh start",' Roger murmured. At Carrie's questioning glance, he explained. 'Koompartoo is aboriginal for "fresh start".'

'It's appropriate, at least.'

Now that her reunion with Oscar was imminent, Carrie's nerves began to jump anew. What would their meeting be like? She was no longer sure she could be cold and distant, as she'd always intended to be if they met again.

Her tension fairly vibrated throughout the car, causing Roger to pat her knee in concern. 'Relax. He's probably as nervous about this meeting as you are.'

She gave him a bleak look. 'How did you guess how I was feeling?'

'Something in the way you're twisting your handkerchief into a rope,' he observed drily.

She looked down at the shredded scrap of cloth in her hand and dropped it into her bag, clenching her hands tightly in her lap. 'The trouble is, I just don't know how I feel about him any more.'

Preoccupied with negotiating the rutted cart track, Roger said, 'So everything's not so cut and dried any more, huh? What made you relent towards Oscar?'

In truth, it was Roger's story about meeting her father years ago that had shown her another side of him. But she didn't want to encourage Roger by admitting how much influence he had over her. So she shrugged. 'Maybe I'm growing up.'

He took his eyes off the road long enough to give her an approving look. 'Maybe you are.'

For some reason, his approval irritated her. 'I'm not going to fall all over him, so don't look so smug,' she said reprovingly. 'He was the one who deserted us, remember?'

The remote look returned at once. 'I'm sure he hasn't forgotten.'

The colony was hidden in jungle and they were among the buildings before they realised they'd arrived at Koompartoo. Krys had given them a description of Oscar's house, which turned out to be the last dwelling in the settlement, on the fringe of the rainforest.

It was built like a pioneer farmhouse, in a basic square with a verandah running all the way around it. The pit-sawn timber slabs looked to be held together by hand-made nails, as if it had been standing since colonial times instead of for just over a decade.

'It looks deserted. Maybe he isn't here,' she said half hopefully. Why on earth had she agreed to come? What could she possibly have to say to him?

There was no more time for thinking. The door of the cottage creaked open and a man emerged, stooping automatically to accommodate his unusual height in the low doorway.

'Dad,' she breathed in an undertone. She felt paralysed, unable to move from her seat in the car.

'Come on. The sooner you get it over with, the better you'll feel,' Roger urged.

Like an automaton, she unbuckled her seat-belt and got out, then forced her legs to carry her the few steps across the compound to the edge of the verandah where her father waited, his face as anxious as her own.

'Caroline, it *is* you!' he said, his reedy voice rising with excitement as he peered closely at her over thick pebble glasses.

The sight of the glasses was her first shock. Her father seemed to have trouble seeing her clearly. 'Yes, it's me,' she said although she couldn't yet bring herself to call him 'Dad' to his face.

She could hardly credit him as the same man she had last seen when she was fourteen. He looked like one of his own caricatures—painfully thin and gaunt so that his bones seemed about to split the weathered parchment skin. His shoulders were narrow and stooped under a shabby checked shirt.

When he removed the thick glasses and massaged his eyes, she saw they were dark caverns in the sun-weathered face. Like her own, his eyes looked grey from a distance, changing to blue close up, with a sunburst of white rays coming from the pupils. Only the fiery light she remembered in them had dimmed.

He replaced his glasses and pulled himself together with an obvious effort. 'Come in, come in. I can hardly believe you're here, Caroline. It's been so long.'

And whose fault was that? she thought angrily, then checked herself. He looked so frail and ill at ease that she just couldn't hurt him the way she had rehearsed it so many times in her youth. Maybe she had grown up, after all.

She turned to Roger, waiting by the car. 'Dad . . . Oscar, this is Roger Torkan, another artist like yourself. We shared the driving coming up here.'

Oscar peered at Roger closely. 'Haven't we met before, young fellow?'

They shook hands. 'I hope so, sir. It was one of the reasons I came—to find out.'

Oscar led the way into the house. After the heat of the sun it was blissfully cool inside. From the verandah, they stepped into what was basically one spacious room. About a third of it was partitioned off into a kitchen area by a heavy timber cabinet. Beside the kitchen was a small bathroom. At the other end of the room was a massive fireplace made from locally hewn granite boulders. Half the ceiling was timbered to create a loft bedroom, accessible by a ladder from the ground floor.

Her father saw her looking around curiously. 'There isn't much in the way of creature comforts, but this is where I live and work.'

'It's charming,' she said and meant it. There was a rustic warmth about the lavish use of timber and the brick floor underfoot, which was strewn with hand-hooked rugs. 'Wherever did you find such superb furniture?'

They were both stalling for time, and she was sure he knew it as well as she did. While father and daughter took stock of each other, he obliged her with an answer. 'Most of this stuff is salvaged. I found the dresser in a community hall in Kempsey which was being pulled down.' He gestured towards the massive timber table taking up the centre of the room. It was strewn with sketches and drawing materials. 'This was an old cutting table I bought at an auction for a dollar. It was covered in layers of felt, but underneath is good solid pine and jarrah.'

At Oscar's urging, they seated themselves around the

table and he cleared a space to set out hand-made ceramic coffee-mugs, which he filled with an aromatic brew, motioning them to help themselves to cream and sugar.

'This is all local produce,' he said, pride in his voice. 'We survive on the barter system here. I grow vegetables and trade them for mushrooms and home-brewed beer or whatever I need. It works very well.' He cleared his throat. 'But you didn't come all the way from Sydney to listen to me waffling on. How've you been, Caroline?'

Suddenly shy, she looked down at her hands. 'Fine. I work . . . worked in the book department of Petrie's in Sydney.'

'Krys told me about your job. Have you given it up then?'

She nodded. 'I'm going back to school to train as a teacher.'

Oscar removed his glasses and fumbled for a handkerchief, then began polishing them. 'That's the best news, lass,' he said huskily. 'Your mother told me how much you wanted to be a teacher. I'm glad you're finally going to make it.'

Wide-eyed, she stared at him. 'Mother told you . . . but . . .'

'You thought we'd been out of touch. I know. Kay told me how much you hated me for leaving so we agreed not to let you know we were writing to each other.'

Roger stood up. 'I'm sure you two have a lot to talk about. Would you mind if I went for a walk around the colony?' He ignored Carrie's frantic look of appeal, keeping his eyes on Oscar.

'Go anywhere you like,' Oscar invited. 'There are no locks on anything, but look out for Gonner.'

Roger's eyebrows drew together. 'Gonner?'

'He's a goanna that got himself run over near here a couple of years ago. We called him that because we thought he was a goner. But he bounced back, and now he's a sort of watch-lizard around the colony.'

Still laughing, Roger went outside, closing the door carefully behind him. Carrie and her father were alone.

There was an awkward silence, then they both opened their mouths at once.

'Caroline, I don't . . .'

'Dad, I can't . . .'

Their laughter broke the tension and they smiled at each other. Oscar gestured generously. 'Ladies first.'

'I don't know where to start. All the things I thought I wanted to say seem unimportant somehow.'

His smile faded. 'You mean you don't want to yell at me, damn me for leaving you—any of those things?'

'Once, I wanted to. I felt so angry and helpless. Now, seeing you here, you seem so much in your element.'

'That's because I am. Your mother recognised it, which is why she asked me to leave when she did—for all our sakes.'

Baffled, she shook her head. 'Wait a minute. Mum *asked* you to leave? Why would she do such a thing?'

'Because she thought my talents, such as they were, shouldn't be lost to the world. I wanted to get a job and support my family decently, but she wouldn't let me do it. She said if I took a job, she would walk out herself and never come back. You girls needed her more than you needed me, so I was the one to move out.

'Kay wasn't qualified for any kind of work, although she tried to get a job. At least with me gone, she qualified for a pension. Then she inherited that monstrous house and fooled us all by making it pay.' His tone was full of admiration. 'I swear to God, I've really tried to justify her faith in me by working from morning to night at the easel. There were times when I've hated the damned thing for taking me away from you all.'

'I still don't understand. Why couldn't you live with us and still draw?'

'How could I shut myself up in a studio while outside, my family went short of everything I should have provided for them? I tried it, but I was torn in so many directions that my work suffered in the end.'

'So you had no choice but to leave.'

He turned shining eyes on her, their grey depths a mirror of her own. 'If you can accept that, can you find it in your heart to forgive me too?'

It was as if a house of cards she had spent half her life building had come tumbling down. 'It'll take me some time to get used to the idea,' she conceded. 'All these years, I've believed you were selfish and irresponsible.'

He rested his thin forearms on the table and studied the worn timber. 'Maybe I am. I could have called Kay's bluff, I suppose, and taken the job over her protests.'

Carrie smiled, thinking of her mother's stubborn nature, which, to a large degree, she had inherited. 'But you know she would have gone, don't you?'

He laughed softly. 'If it killed her.'

At long last, she felt a sense of kinship with her father, as she marvelled at the sacrifice his pictures in the National Gallery represented. For the first time, she felt stirrings of pride in him. 'I'm glad you told me the truth,' she said, her eyes glistening. 'I've wasted so much time.'

He patted her hand reassuringly. 'You're here now, love, that's what matters.' For the umpteenth time, he removed the thick glasses and massaged his deep-set eyes, which were ringed with violet shadows.

She watched him in concern, at first thinking he might be overcome by emotion, as she was herself. Then she realised that there was another problem. 'Is something the matter with your eyes?' she asked.

'Nothing anyone can help, I'm afraid. They're just plain worn out.'

Sudden fear gripped her. 'If it's a medical problem, there's a lot they can do these days. Laser surgery . . .' She tailed off.

Sadly, he shook his head. 'I've looked into it carefully, love. The eye specialist tells me there's some haemorrhaging in the blood vessels at the back of my eyes. I've had treatment but it hasn't helped. I have to face the fact that I'll lose my sight altogether in time.'

This time, the term came easily to her lips. 'Oh, Dad!'

He smiled wanly. 'It's almost worth it to hear you call me that again. Don't worry about me, love, I've had a good life, done a lot of work—hopefully, some of it will endure after me. For Kay's sake, I pray it will anyway.'

'Does she know?' Her voice came out in a whisper.

'She knows I'm having problems, but I haven't told her the worst of it. I want her to worry about herself, for a change, instead of always putting me first.'

But blindness! The idea of him living alone here, robbed of his sight and his ability to work was too horrible to contemplate. 'Come back to Sydney and live with Krys and me,' she said impulsively.

This time, the mistiness in his eyes was from emotion and he gripped her hand convulsively. 'The offer alone means more than I can tell you, Caroline. But my home is here, among my friends and the birds and animals. Even old Gonner's a friend, and comes to me for titbits. Besides, what about when you and Krys get married?

You won't want an old fool like me around your neck.'
He leaned forward, his expression crafty. 'Tell me
about this young man of yours, Roger.'

She felt her cheeks heating. 'He isn't my young man.
He came with me because he thinks you two met out in
the bush when he was a teenager. You inspired him to
take up art as a career.'

'So that colour in your face is joy at us being brought
back together, is it?' he asked shrewdly. 'My eyesight
isn't so bad that I can't recognise a good old-fashioned
blush, young lady. Are you in love with him?'

'He wants to marry me,' she said, evading his
question.

'So what's stopping you?' he asked pointedly.

Her face lit up with a sudden realisation. 'Nothing.
Nothing at all.' And there wasn't. All these years, she
had believed that marriage to an artist like Oscar meant
endless struggle and sacrifice. Now she knew the real
reason why he left them, she knew it didn't have to be
like that. Unlike Kay, she was quite capable of
supporting them both while Roger worked at his art.

It wouldn't matter if he had no head for business—
she would have. Now she knew that artists weren't
necessarily selfish and irresponsible, she could see a
future for them, provided Roger wasn't chauvinistic
about who earned their keep. And surely he wouldn't
mind?

She turned her shining gaze towards the front door,
which had swung open while they talked. Roger stood
framed in the opening and straight away she noticed a
handkerchief wrapped around his left thumb.

'What's the matter? Are you hurt?' she asked in
alarm.

He grinned ruefully. 'I met Gonner. He bites.'

Oscar removed the makeshift bandage, clucking

over the small wound. 'It's not serious. Gonner takes his sentry duties too much to heart sometimes. I hope you're up to date with your tetanus shots?'

'Yes, I am, luckily.' He saw Carrie's frightened face and winked at her. 'Don't worry, it's only a scratch. Gonner's the one who's likely to get food poisoning from fastening on to me.'

All the same, she wasn't happy until he had rinsed the wound and bathed it in antiseptic. When they were finally able to sit down again, Roger and Oscar exchanged looks which clearly said, 'Women!'

This time, Oscar poured them each a glass of a locally made fruit wine, which was light and fragrant, although heady, he warned them, if one drank too much.

'Now, Roger,' he said after they'd sampled their wine, 'tell me about this historic meeting you and I had.'

Roger refreshed his memory about the meeting in the bush years ago, and about Oscar's role in his becoming a cartoonist.

'So "Emily" is your creation, then? It's syndicated in one of the Kempsey papers,' Oscar explained. 'I'm usually about a week behind on my newspapers, but I always get a laugh out of Emily's antics. That Lucy you've had move in with Emily is a real character.'

As Carrie twisted uncomfortably in her seat, she realised that her father's failing eyesight had made him overlook the resemblance. She wondered if Roger had guessed.

'It's kind of you to say so,' he told Oscar, looking pointedly at Carrie. 'Not everyone shares your enthusiasm.'

'Like some of my stuff,' Oscar agreed. 'They ask me when I'm going to do some real work, like oils, instead of this childish black and white scribble.'

The two men discussed art for a while, then talked about the pieces Oscar would contribute to Krys's exhibition. Since in some ways it was a retrospective look at Pop Art over the last twenty years to the present, Oscar decided on a selection of drawings that would highlight the evolution of his cartooning style.

Listening to Roger, Carrie was even happier that he had accompanied her on this trip. She would have been at a loss as to which drawings to take back for Krys. Come to that, Krys herself would have been more able to make the selection, although she claimed to lack the time to come. Had she known how Carrie would react when she heard Oscar's side of the story? Maybe this was what she'd had in mind all along.

A grudging admiration for her sister crept over Carrie. She had always seen herself as the role model for Krys but it seemed she herself could learn a few things from her younger sister.

It was dusk by the time everything was loaded into the back of Carrie's car. Oscar was full of apologies for being unable to offer them a bed for the night.

'This is strictly bachelor accommodation,' he explained. 'I don't even have a couch you could sleep on, although Carrie would be welcome to have my bed.'

She kissed him impetuously. 'Don't be silly. I wouldn't dream of putting you out of your bed. There are dozens of motels in Kempsey so we're sure to get a room ... rooms,' she added quickly.

Oscar gave her an indulgent look. 'Maybe you were right the first time, love.' He leaned forward, directing his words to her ear. 'He's a fine bloke, Caroline. If anybody can make this work, you can. Your mother and I worked out the only solution we could, but maybe you'll think of a better one. You have my blessing, anyway.'

Tears threatened to choke her again as she hugged him goodbye. 'Thanks, Dad,' she whispered and saw his gratified smile as they got into the car for the drive back to Kempsey.

In the failing light, the drive down the mountain was tortuously slow. Roger turned the headlights on full, catching dozens of kangaroos in their glare. They gazed back at the car with startled eyes, then bounded off into the dark bush on either side of the road.

When they were nearly back at the highway again, Roger risked a look at her. 'Glad you came?'

Dumbly, she nodded, then realised that he couldn't see the gesture in the dark car. 'Yes, I am.'

'He's a splendid man, your father. One day, you should go and see his work in Canberra.'

'I think I might.'

'I'm glad I had the chance to thank him for all he did for me,' Roger went on. 'If it hadn't been for his encouragement, I might be a frustrated lawyer today.'

'Instead of the man I love,' she said softly.

The car swerved, the headlights dancing off the ghostly eucalyptus trees at the roadside, until Roger brought the car sharply under control again. There was a screech of rubber as he slowed and came to a stop, the tyres crunching on gravel at the roadside. Then, he slammed on the handbrake and turned to her impatiently. 'What did you just say?'

She repeated it in a barely audible whisper and gasped as he pulled her towards him. 'Do you really mean that, Carrie?'

'Oh, yes, Roger. Maybe seeing my father again today shook something loose in me, but I finally faced the fact—I love you, and nothing else matters.'

She could imagine his shining expression, although

his face was a silhouette against the night sky. 'My God, Carrie, you don't know how happy you've just made me!'

Before she could say any more, he tore at the seatbelts separating them, and drew her into his arms so she was half across his lap. Then his mouth was on hers, his breath hot and tasting of the fruit wine they'd both drunk at Oscar's. Gently, he parted her lips and touched his tongue to hers, sending jets of flame all through her body. One hand caressed the back of her neck while the other was hot and demanding as it roved over her thigh, burning her skin through her jeans.

She wound her arms around his wide shoulders, revelling in the resistance her fingers met from the muscle and sinew that tautened the fabric of his shirt. Then, he took her hand and guided it down his body until she felt a throbbing hardness under her fingers.

She pulled her hand away as if scorched, and he crushed her against him. 'Carrie, this means you will marry me, doesn't it?'

'Of course,' she answered simply, aware that her own desire was now as aroused as his. 'Oh, Roger, I love you so much.' It was heaven to be able to confess it at last.

With an oath of impatience, he pulled away from her and clamped both hands on the steering wheel. 'We're nearly at Kempsey,' he said, his voice vibrant with desire for her. 'Did you mean it when you said we would get a room—singular—or was that a slip of the tongue?'

'It must have been a Freudian slip,' she confessed, her chest muscles tightening as she contemplated what he was suggesting. The idea of putting even a flimsy hotel wall between them was suddenly unendurable. 'Yes, I meant a room, singular, darling.'

His breath was expelled in a long, controlled gasp. 'Then let's get the hell out of here.'

CHAPTER EIGHT

It was late by the time they reached Kempsey and many of the hotels had No Vacancy signs up. At last, they found a place in Belgrave Street, not far from the main shopping centre, where accommodation was still available.

It was quaintly called The Digger's Rest, but it was actually a modern ranch-style complex set in spacious grounds. The rooms opened on to a central courtyard and had balconies overlooking a pool and spa.

Although Carrie felt acutely self-conscious, the desk clerk looked uninterested when Roger gave his name and requested a double room. Without asking, the clerk scribbled down 'Mr and Mrs Torkan' and handed a key to Roger.

Mr and Mrs Torkan. A frisson of excitement surged through her. How wonderful it sounded! Soon it would be a reality—tonight, in fact, she added to herself, suppressing a rush of apprehension. The ceremony they would go through later couldn't make any difference to the commitment they felt for each other now.

Still, her apprehension persisted. Roger was so much more worldly than she was. How could she ever hope to satisfy a man like him?

'Not having second thoughts?' he asked as they explored their room a few minutes later.

'No, this is fine,' she said, averting her eyes from the enormous bed that took up the centre of the room.

He dropped the suitcases and was at her side in two strides, turning her until she was in his arms. 'I want

you more than I've ever wanted any woman,' he
confessed in husky tones, 'but I can wait if you want me
to.' He cupped her chin in his hand and tilted her face
up to his. 'Only tell me now, because once I start kissing
you, I may not be able to give you the choice.'

Once he started kissing her . . . the promise alone was
enough to start a fierce tingling sensastion in the pit of
her stomach. She looked up at him with wide, trusting
eyes. 'I love you, Roger.'

It wasn't an answer, yet it was all the answer he
needed. With a groan, he crushed her to him and bent
his head until their lips met. If his touch had excited her
in the car, his kiss now electrified them both and she
surrendered to the sensations willingly. His arms were
around her shoulders. Gradually, his hands slid lower
until he cupped her hips, pulling her tighter against him
until she could feel his unmistakable desire. The
discovery heightened her own growing excitement.

All the time, his lips roved over her face, covering
her with kisses as if to brand her as his own. When he
stopped for breath, she nestled her head into the crook
of his shoulder, breathing in his musky male scent,
which was still tinged with a faint spiciness from the
aftershave he had used in the morning.

'You smell nice,' she murmured.

'So do you,' he rejoined, his voice muffled against her
hair. 'All rich and warm, like fresh-cut flowers.'

'"Sugar and spice and all things nice",' she quoted,
drugged by the strength of the passions he was arousing
in her. 'Except that I'm not a little girl.'

'I hope to God you aren't,' he ground out, lifting her
off her feet.

Before she could react, he placed her carefully on the
bed. But the gallant effect was spoiled when she
bounced up and down unexpectedly.

Helplessly, she broke into peals of laughter. 'It's a water bed!'

He tested it with his hand. 'So it is. I hope you're a good sailor.'

'I've never slept in one before.'

'There's a first time for everything,' he said ambiguously. He began to strip off his shirt with economical movements revealing his massively male shoulders and hair-strewn chest fully to her for the first time.

She drew a deep breath of admiration. What a magnificent-looking man he was. She laughed suddenly.

He paused. 'Now what's so funny?'

'I was remembering the first words I said to you,' she said, her eyes dancing. 'How could I have thought for a minute that you might be gay?'

He continued undressing. 'Those are words I now intend to make you eat, my girl.'

She laughed in delighted anticipation, all doubts swept away by his ease and assurance. How could she be nervous when he was so obviously at ease with her? She tried to stand up so she could get undressed herself, but she only floundered helplessly on the heaving surface.

'Help me up—please?' she begged, trying unsuccessfully to right herself.

His eyes roved over her long-limbed form, spreadeagled on the bed, and he smiled languorously. 'Why should I, when I have you where I want you?'

'Because I'm not much good to you fully dressed,' she retorted, then felt a wave of heat wash over her. There must have been a love potion in Oscar's fruit wine—she had never behaved so . . . so wantonly before.

Roger knelt beside her, keeping his balance much

more successfully than she had. 'I can see you need help,' he breathed.

She looked quickly away, holding her breath as he began to undress her where she lay.

It wasn't the easiest task, removing her shirt and form-fitting jeans while she was lying down, but Roger managed it with a skill which afforded her a twinge of concern. Wasn't he a little *too* good at this? Then she told herself she was worrying needlessly. A man like Roger was bound to have a past—but he had made it clear she was his present and future, and that was all she cared about.

At last they were both naked and there was no more time for talk. Taking her in his arms, Roger rolled with her to the centre of the bed but it had developed its own momentum under them.

'It's like a roller coaster,' she gasped. When he leaned forward to kiss her, the bed plunged downwards creating a trough on her side and a tidal wave on his.

'It won't be so bad if we try to catch the same wave,' he grinned. To prove his point, he clutched her hard against him so they moved up and down in unison.

His kisses stirred every nerve ending to vibrant life. Suddenly, the wallowing motion didn't matter any more. She was too intent on the internal roller coaster ride he was taking her on, as they exchanged kisses and caresses with growing excitement.

Although it was exquisite torment to delay her fulfilment any longer, she forced herself to slow her breathing and her racing heartbeat, marvelling at nature's generosity in creating him for her. It was hardly fair that one man should have so many advantages. He had the body of a male model, all lean planes and angles, and he was tanned to a golden hue all over, save for the white patch where his swimming trunks came.

His face she already knew so well, and, as she kissed his brow tenderly, she delighted afresh in the sexy ambivalence of a brooding male profile combined with a little-boy smile. Those arresting bluer-than-blue eyes were closed now, his breathing was short and shallow, as he rolled towards her, opening his eyes and mesmerising her in their glare. 'You're a witch,' he breathed. 'I can't take any more of this.'

'Then why . . .' she began but her question was muffled by his mouth covering hers, while his body followed suit. She opened her arms to him gladly, desiring him more than she would have believed possible.

The whole world might have ceased to exist as their awareness spiralled in on each other. They were no longer two people but one perfect whole, two heart-beats throbbing in the most perfect union. They were the last survivors on earth, then they, too, exploded into the cosmos, in a supernova of light and fiery warmth. Moments later, the world was miraculously restored to them and they smiled at each other, sharing their secrets in silence. They had travelled to a far universe together and returned full of wonder at what they had found.

As she lay cradled in the crook of his arm, the bed finally calming beneath them, Carrie thought she had never felt so blissfully happy. It was as if part of her had always been missing, only now being restored to her.

Very carefully, so as not to start the wave-motion up again, she eased her head around and looked at Roger. The little-boy look was back as he slept, but she knew now it was pure illusion. There was nothing boyish about him. He was all man—her man. She sighed contentedly.

She must have slept more deeply than she anticipated, because it was full daylight by the time she opened her eyes. The space beside her was empty, and her rush of alarm was allayed when she heard the splash of the shower in the adjoining bathroom.

Indulgently, she focused on the sound, noticing that Roger was also singing. Off-key, admittedly, but then you couldn't have everything! This was what every morning would be like after they were married, she told herself dreamily. Only she would be the one dashing off to work, while he adjourned to his studio in their home, to draw his cartoons.

She told him about her plans over breakfast which they ate on the balcony of their suite, overlooking the pool. At this hour, the pool was empty and the sunlight sparkled off the azure water like strands of diamonds.

'Do you think it'll work?' she asked him anxiously.

He smiled, although she had the uncomfortable feeling that he was humouring her. 'I don't see why not, if that's the way you want it.'

She pouted prettily. 'You're teasing me.'

He spread his hands wide, his expression deceptively innocent. 'No, I'm not. I'm agreeing with you.' He folded his arms across his expansive chest. 'In fact, I rather like the idea of you going off to your daily grind while I stay home and commune with my muse.' He passed the back of his hand across his forehead in a theatrical gesture and she was forced to laugh.

'Idiot! But it will work, I know it will.' She sobered abruptly. 'If only Mum had been able to support our family, we wouldn't have had to split up.'

Roger frowned. 'You don't know for sure that it would have made any difference. Maybe Oscar just wasn't the type to divide himself between a family and his work.'

'But he said ...'

'I know, you told me what he said. But just because he told you what you wanted to hear, it doesn't mean it would have worked in fact.'

Unhappily, she traced a pattern in the butter on her toast with her knife. 'Are you saying it won't work for us?'

He clucked his tongue impatiently. 'Why must you always have everything so cut and dried? I thought, after your decision about your job, that you were developing a spirit of adventure.'

'Last night was an adventure for me,' she said softly. She took a sip of her orange juice. 'Was it an adventure for you, too?' She thought again of her fear that she was one of many where he was concerned.

He sensed her anxiety. 'Yes, it was a wonderful adventure,' he assured her. 'The start of a lifetime of them, if you still feel the same way.'

Was he as unsure of her as she was of him? 'Of course I do,' she said. 'I already know what you mean to me, Roger. Any ceremony will be an anti-climax for me.'

'You mean you'd live with me if I asked you to, without benefit of clergy as the saying goes?'

Her spirits plummeted. Surely he wouldn't ask that of her? Then she remembered her resolution to let nothing stand in the way of their happiness, and she raised her head defiantly. 'Yes, if you want me to.'

In an instant, he left his chair and pulled her from hers to enfold her in a tight embrace. 'You crazy little fool; I just wanted to find out how much I meant to you.'

'Then you still want to marry me?' she asked, her voice choked.

'Of course, as soon as possible.' He kissed her again, heedless of who might be watching, and the wildfire that tore along her veins made her so responsive that she didn't care either.

Suddenly, he pulled away. 'Do we have to go back to Sydney today?'

'Not really. Krys said there was no need to hurry.' She smiled in wonder. 'You don't think that little schemer planned this whole thing, do you?'

'Krys as matchmaker, you mean? She might with a little expert guidance.'

Suddenly understanding, she beat her fists against his chest. 'You devil! You put her up to this trip, didn't you? Why, I'll bet you even planted the idea of the gallery using some of Oscar's work!'

His chastened expression was her answer and he looked more than ever like a small boy, this time one caught with his hand in the cookie jar. 'Can you forgive me for it?'

She pretended to consider it. 'I might, at a price.'

He didn't need to ask what her price was. As one, they left the breakfast things and went back inside to the water bed, where he paid her more handsomely than she could have asked.

Afterwards, as they lay on the gently moving surface, she said, 'What shall we do today?'

He grinned at her. 'I thought we already did it.'

She started to pummel his ribs but the movement of the bed carried her almost over the side until he grabbed her around the waist. 'That will teach you to get violent.'

In desperation, she jumped off the bed and sat in one of the padded armchairs across the room, watching him rise and fall on the bed in the wake of her departure. 'We can't spend all day in here,' she said firmly, rising. 'Why don't we go exploring, find a deserted beach somewhere and . . .'

'If we're going to do that we may as well stay right here,' he teased.

She averted her eyes, marvelling at how he could make such intimate jokes so lightly. 'I was going to say . . . and have a picnic,' she said primly.

He sighed melodramatically. 'If that's what the lady wants!'

She had to insist, even though every instinct urged her to rejoin him on the water bed. As far as she was concerned, their marriage had already begun so they should start as they meant to go on. Which meant behaving responsibly, for one thing. Unlike her mother, she wasn't going to let Roger set the rules and have them while away their days in indolence. Already she felt guilty about agreeing to delay their return to Sydney by a day. There would be no more such behaviour once they were married.

After some discussion, they agreed to drive north to visit the ruins of the historic Trial Bay Gaol. The handsome old settlement was built of grey granite quarried nearby; and stood on a headland overlooking a picturesque half moon of beach that stretched for miles.

With the exception of the breakwater built by convicts in 1870, the bay looked much as it did when Captain Cook christened the nearby Smoky Cape during his discovery of Australia in 1770.

'It's so tranquil, yet it must have been a grim sight to the poor souls interned there,' she said looking at the walled settlemnt.

Hand in hand, they inspected the ruins and the polished granite obelisk nearby. Every time Roger clasped his hands around her waist to lift her over some obstacle, Carrie felt a thrill surge through her. A group of young women tourists looked at him admiringly and murmured among themselves, causing Carrie to draw unconsciously closer to him. Far from being jealous of the way the other women eyed Roger, she was elated to be the one he had chosen.

Only a few miles further on at the mouth of the Macleay River, was the fishing village of South West Rocks, where they decided to stop for lunch. 'You know what I'd like to eat?' Roger said nostalgically.

'No. What?'

'A parcel of fresh prawns from the fishing co-op. I haven't peeled and eaten them out of newspaper since I was a boy around here.'

They had already inspected the fleet of small boats and trawlers that plied the bay and surrounding reefs, and the air was redolent of fresh fish. Carrie's mouth began to water. 'Then we can find that deserted beach and . . .'

'. . . have a picnic!' they chorused as one.

They bought some rosy-red cooked prawns as large as sausages and drove back to Smoky Cape where they could enjoy the view of the rugged coastline to the north and south as they ate.

Roger had bought a small bottle of Hunter Valley Riesling and he poured the chilled wine into the plastic cups Carrie kept in her car. He lifted his in a toast. 'To us.'

Her eyes danced as she returned the gesture. 'To us.'

Her gaze went to his fingers as he carefully removed the head and tail of a large prawn, then de-veined and peeled it skilfully. How strong and capable his hands were! Her throat went dry as she recalled the feel of his caresses last night and this morning.

Gulping, she bent her head and tried to concentrate on peeling her share of king prawns.

To quell the desires surging through her errant body,

she said the first thing that came into her head. 'Now you'll be able to introduce me to your illustrious relative, Gil Marten.'

He finished peeling a prawn before he answered. 'You'll make me jealous if you sound too eager.'

She turned shining eyes to him. 'After last night you must know you have nothing to fear from him, however successful he is.'

He nodded soberly. 'All the same, after Krys's exhibition will be soon enough to let you meet him.'

'Will he be at the opening, then?' She recalled Krys saying that some of Marten's work was to be featured, to her sister's joy.

'Yes, but he's camera shy so you won't spot him until I point him out to you.'

She nodded agreement, but found she no longer cared about meeting the famous artist. The only man she cared about was here with her. Even her fears of the future were starting to recede now she had decided to take the reins of their future into her own hands.

Roger had suggested much more than a picnic and she never knew how they avoided making love there on the beach. His every gesture and touch set her body alight with desire. Only her own resolution kept her out of his arms until it was time to return to The Digger's Rest.

They were almost back at Kempsey when they heard the shriek of a police siren behind them.

Carrie clutched Roger's arm. 'Are you speeding?'

He glanced at the speedometer. 'No, we're well within the limits. And one glass of wine with lunch hasn't affected my driving.' He shrugged and slowed down, pulling over to the grass verge as the police car drew in ahead of them.

Carrie wound her side window down and looked out

at the officer looming over her. 'Miss Caroline Doyle?'

Baffled, she nodded. 'Yes.'

'We've been looking for you. Do you have a sister, Krystine?'

'Oh my God, nothing's happened to Krys?'

'No, she's fine. She was the one who got in touch with us. I'm afraid it's still bad news. Your mother was taken to hospital this morning after a heart attack. This was the only way your sister could think to reach you, since she didn't know where you were staying. We've been on the lookout for your car.'

Carrie barely heard the explanation. She was too dazed by the verbal blow the policeman had just delivered. Her mother—ill? Perhaps dying at this very minute. She gripped Roger's arm more tightly. 'I've got to get back.'

He nodded tautly. 'I'll drive you to the airport. I can return your car and belongings later.'

They had forgotten the policeman still standing there until he said, 'I'm afraid there's no direct flight from Kempsey to Sydney at this time of year—no landing lights here, so it's strictly a daylight airport I'm afraid.' Seeing Carrie's stricken expression, he added quickly, 'But there is a coach to Port Macquarie, which connects with a flight from there. It takes about two hours all up, which is a lot quicker than driving.' He consulted his watch. 'If I give you an escort to the airport, you'll be in plenty of time for the evening flight.'

He was as good as his word, clearing a path for them through the light evening traffic all the way to the airport. Carrie was in no mood to appreciate the experience, however, being too preoccupied with worry about her mother.

Only when Roger came to help her aboard the waiting coach did she realise what her quick return must mean. 'I hate to leave you,' she said, her eyes misty.

He hugged her tightly. 'Don't be silly. I'll be back in Sydney tomorrow and I'll come straight to your place to see how your mother's doing. I'll bring Oscar's pictures and your luggage with me.'

She had almost forgotten the reason for their trip. 'Thanks,' she said distractedly. He kissed her quickly but possessively and it was an effort to wrench herself from his arms to climb aboard the coach.

The sight of Roger standing alone beside the coach tore at her already ragged nerves. Leaving him was like leaving a part of herself behind, yet she was anxious to reach her mother's side before ... before ... she couldn't complete the thought.

The drive to Port Macquarie and the flight to Sydney passed in a blur. One minute, the trip seemed endless, and the next it rushed past too quickly, giving her no time to adjust.

It was just over two hours later when the taxi deposited her at her flat, where the policeman had told her Krys would wait for her. The television was playing quietly, but Krys was curled up in an armchair sound asleep. Carrie's heart went out to her. She was reluctant to wake her sister but she had to know more about their mother.

When shaken gently, Krys stirred, then her eyes fluttered open and she looked up at her sister. 'Oh, Carrie, I'm so sorry.'

Carrie's heart turned over in her chest and she staggered to the other armchair. 'Oh, God, Krys!'

Krys sat up at once, horrified at the impression she had created. 'No, Carrie, it isn't anything like that. Mum's fine. I meant I'm sorry for dragging you back here like this. It ... it turned out to be a false alarm.'

'Mum's really all right?' Carrie's voice was no more than a strangled whisper.

'Yes, she's fine, honestly. I was half asleep or I wouldn't have given you any other impression. Her doctor thought at first it was a heart attack, and rushed her to hospital, so I panicked and asked the police to get a message to you.'

She looked so abject that Carrie forced herself to smile, although her nerves were so ragged she felt more like bursting into tears. 'It's all right, you weren't to know. Go on, please.'

'The hospital did some tests and they found she has an irregular heartbeat. They think she may have had a mild heart attack some time in the past, but dismissed it as something else.'

'Poor Mum,' Carrie said. 'Have they kept her in hospital?'

'They're keeping her in overnight for observation. Then they want her to have complete rest and quiet for a while. Although she didn't have a real heart attack this time, they fear she could if she doesn't take better care of herself.'

'How is she to rest with the demands of running Megalong?' Carrie asked bleakly. She was assailed by guilt. Her mother had tried to discuss her problems, but Carrie had been too preoccupied over Roger to worry about anyone else.

Krys looked away. 'She wanted to tell you herself, but I think you should know, Mum's decided to sell Megalong.'

'She talked about it last time I was up in the mountains,' said Carrie. 'She told me it was becoming too big a strain, but I didn't realise just how bad things were.'

Krys smiled, remembering. 'Mum was never one to

complain about anything, was she? Why, she never
once said a word against Dad—and heaven help
anyone else who tried to.'

Knowing what had happened between Oscar and
Kay, Carrie was much more understanding. 'When can
I see Mum?' she asked.

Krys brightened. 'Tomorrow, if you like. I've
suggested she should come and stay with us for a while
after she's discharged.'

'That's a good idea. I'll share with you and she can
have my room.'

Krys frowned. 'The only problem is, how to stop her
worrying about Megalong while she rests.'

'I have the solution. I've done all I can to help you
with your exhibition, and Roger will deliver Oscar's
sketches to you tomorrow. So there's nothing to stop me
going up to the mountains to mind the house until
Mum's better. She can plan the sale in her own good
time, without having to worry about her guests in the
meantime.'

'I don't deserve you, Carrie,' her mother laughed, when
Carrie told her the plan at the hospital next day.
'Whatever would I do without you both?'

Carrie refrained from reminding her that without the
encumbrance of two daughters, her life would have
been much easier in the first place. 'You've done a lot
for us,' she said. 'Now it's our turn.'

Obviously relieved, Kay settled back against her
pillows. 'Now, tell me all about Oscar.'

This was the moment Carrie had been dreading,
even without the added strain of her mother's delicate
health. How could she tell Kay about Oscar's failing
sight? 'He was very cheerful,' she said carefully.

'And how are his eyes?' her mother asked shrewdly.

'His ... his eyes?'

'I know he's been having problems. I'd have known even without him telling me, because his handwriting has been getting steadily worse with every letter.' She looked keenly at her daughter, reading a lot into her silence. 'You've got to tell me the truth, Carrie. It's worse than he's told me, isn't it?'

She nodded miserably. 'He's going blind.'

Kay screwed up her eyes in pain. 'The fool! Why didn't he tell me?'

'He didn't want to worry you, I suppose.'

'He's been worrying me since the day we met but somehow, I've never learned how to stop loving him.' She smiled through a veil of tears. 'What a fool you must think me, darling.'

Shaking her head, Carrie perched on the side of the bed and took her mother's hand. 'Quite the opposite, Mum. After the long talk I had with Dad, I can understand how you feel. He is kind of attractive, isn't he?'

Kay beamed. 'It does my heart good to hear you admit it, darling. I know our life hasn't been easy for you.'

'Harder for you,' Carrie reminded her.

'But at least it was my own choice. You didn't ask to be born to such a screwy couple.'

So Mum still thought of herself and Oscar as a couple! The idea made Carrie's heart sing. 'You aren't screwy,' she said firmly, 'you're just you.' Hesitantly, she went on to tell Kay about her love for Roger, which was in many ways a carbon copy of her parents' love affair.

Kay hugged her. 'I'm so happy for you darling. From what you've told me about your Roger, he is a very special person.'

'Which is why I love him so much,' Carrie assured her dreamily. 'We plan to announce our engagement right after the opening of Krys's exhibition. It wouldn't be fair beforehand, since this occasion means so much to her. I hope you'll keep Megalong long enough for us to be married there?'

'Of course I will.' She looked thoughtfully out of the window at the verdant hospital grounds. 'You know, it will be a relief to be rid of it after all these years. It was such a godsend when your great-aunt left it to me out of the blue, but it has become a millstone around my neck.'

'Krys and I should have realised how you felt and done more to help.'

'Nonsense. You two have your own lives to live.'

Carrie hugged her mother again. 'Did I ever tell you you're the best mother in the world?'

Her mother cocked an eye at the heart monitor beeping steadily over her bed. 'To think I had to land in here to get you to admit it!'

Carrie had finally broached her career plans with Krys, who was delighted. Now, she shared them with her mother who was every bit as pleased. They were still discussing the idea when there was a knock on the door. It opened to admit Roger, looking tired after his long drive back from Kempsey. The fatigued look dropped away and his face lit up when he saw Carrie at her mother's bedside.

'Krys told me where to find you,' he explained. 'How are you, Mrs Doyle?'

Carrie introduced them, and soon the two people she loved most in the world were laughing and chatting like old friends. She watched them fondly, content to be left out of the conversation so she could watch the two of them.

'So you're going to be away in the mountains for a couple of weeks playing guesthouse *concierge*?' he said when the situation was explained to him.

Something twisted deep inside her. How ever was she to do without him even for such a short time? 'You can come up and stay for a few days, can't you?' she appealed, no longer concerned about appearances. Her mother must have guessed the extent of their involvement as soon as she saw the way they looked at each other. As it was, their hands kept wandering towards each other as if drawn by magnets.

Roger looked uncomfortable. 'I may not be able to,' he said, surprisng her. 'You see, I'll have a lot of work to do with ... with "Emily" over the next couple of weeks.'

'You could always come and work at Megalong. There's loads of room,' she offered.

'Thanks, but I work best on my own,' he said shortly. 'I'll be close by because I'll be involved in the Glenfield exhibition.'

Oh, yes, he had time for Krys, his protégée, but not for Carrie, his future bride. 'You don't have to explain,' she said a little stiffly. Was his work already driving a wedge between them, as her father's had between her parents? 'I understand.'

At her embittered tone, he seemed tempted to say something more, then his eyes retreated into narrow slits, a sure sign of his annoyance with her. Then he took his leave of Kay and gave Carrie a perfunctory kiss on her forehead. 'I'll be in touch,' he said again.

Don't say it unless you mean it, she wanted to scream at his departing back. But she bit the words back. Why wouldn't he come and work at Megalong so they could be together? It was only for two weeks. Surely a cartoonist could work almost anywhere?

There had to be another reason, one he wasn't willing to share with her. The only one she could think of was so painful she shrank from expressing it even to herself—that he simply didn't want to come. Having got what he wanted from her on the pretext of wanting to marry her, he now wanted out.

What would she do if it was true?

CHAPTER NINE

SHE had little time to brood over Roger's strange behaviour. For the next few days, her hands were full looking after Megalong in Kay's absence.

How ever had her mother managed so well for so long? she wondered as she cleaned her fourth bathroom that morning. A cook and a maid were employed casually, but there was still a great deal of work left for Carrie to do.

The run-down condition of the century-old house made every chore doubly difficult. Perched atop one of the great cliffs overlooking the Megalong Valley, the house boasted nine guest bedrooms, each with a massive brass bedstead and porcelain hand basin. There were also several antiquated bathrooms, each with a distinctive leaded glass panel over the door. All of it had to be meticulously maintained.

The dining-room was Carrie's nemesis, requiring hours to dust and vacuum. It was huge and high ceilinged, with carved oak panels around the walls and a musician's gallery overhead, although this was now used for storage.

Being open to the public, the dining-room was the most used part of the great house, and Kay had acquired a reputation for serving nostalgic foods such as creamed cauliflower soup, rack of lamb with rosemary, and home-made ice cream with triangles of wafer biscuit.

As she paused in her dusting, Carrie was forced to admire the way her mother had built Megalong up from a run-down old mansion into a successful business and tourist attraction. She would get a good price for it when she sold up.

The idea saddened Carrie every time she thought about it. Megalong was the only real home she'd known. Even though the family apartment was dark and cramped, as girls she and Krys had revelled in the freedom of the spacious grounds with the gigantic old pine trees, and gravel that crunched invitingly underfoot.

She looked around, her gaze blurring. She would miss the old place with its red and gilt opulence. With an effort, she dismissed the wave of nostalgia. Her mother deserved her chance at happiness, and if selling Megalong would give it to her then the sooner she put it on the market, the better.

Carrie was sure her mother meant to go and live with Oscar at Koompartoo. She welcomed the prospect, although she knew it would be a big step for her mother, living in a rustic artists' colony after the shabby elegance of Megalong.

'Penny for them,' said a familiar voice.

With a start, she looked up as Bianca West came into the dining-room. Carrie stared at the woman as if seeing an apparition, before she scrambled to her feet. 'Hello. This is a surprise!' And not a pleasant one, she could have added, but held her tongue.

'I was driving through Blackheath and I decided to stop for lunch.' She looked around the deserted room. 'You *are* open for lunch, aren't you?'

'I'm afraid not. These days we only serve breakfast to the residents, and open the dining-room to the public for dinner.'

Bianca moved further into the room, the silk of her full-skirted red dress swirling in graceful folds around her slender legs. 'What a pity.'

She didn't sound disappointed at all, Carrie reflected, wondering if the woman had known all along that they weren't open. Maybe it was just an excuse to come in and look around. 'Can I help you with something else?' she enquired, forcing herself to sound polite.

Bianca settled into one of the velvet-covered chairs as if she fully intended to stay for a while. Evidently she didn't consider herself part of the general public. 'You don't mind if I rest a few moments. It's so lovely and cool in here.' She fluttered her eyelashes provocatively.

The effect was wasted on Carrie, although she wasn't sure it would have been, had she been a man. 'Of course not, make yourself at home.' She added churlishly, 'I hope you won't mind if I go on with my work, though.'

Bianca laughed lightly. 'You know what they say: "Work fascinates me, I can sit and look at it for hours".'

'I'm sure you can,' Carrie muttered *sotto voce*, giving all her attention to dusting the carved oak servery.

'My mother used to come to places like this when the Blue Mountains were in their heyday,' Bianca mused. 'They all came, you know, royalty, politicians, tycoons, society matrons—mother was one of those. I'd give a lot to have seen it—the gentlemen in their silk shirts and tails and the ladies in their magnificent gowns. There would have been a string quartet playing in that gallery, then.'

She sounded genuinely nostalgic, Carrie realised in surprise. She wouldn't have thought Bianca West had a romantic bone in her beautiful body. 'I suppose it must have been marvellous,' she found herself agreeing. 'Instead of whizzing through in a fast car, one would have journeyed by carriage, stopping for a Devonshire cream tea and croquet on the lawns.'

'Just think, if Roger had lived here then, he would have worked from a little sandstone cottage in the foothills, like Norman Lindsay's place near Springwood,' Bianca went on.

If she was surprised to hear Roger's name coming so easily from Bianca's lips, Carrie was careful not to show it. Their engagement wouldn't become public knowledge until after Krys's opening so she couldn't say very much. 'Roger and Norman Lindsay would have been kindred spirits,' she said, 'Lindsay was quite a controversial cartoonist in his day, although he also painted and sketched, as well as making model ships and sculptures.'

'Oh, but Roger is quite versatile,' Bianca trilled. 'The reason I came up here today was to look at a wall mural he painted on a house in Katoomba. He's going to do one for my Hunters Hill place.'

'You've asked him to?'

'Not yet, but we understand each other so there's no problem. Why only last night, he was saying . . .'

It was out before she could prevent it. 'You saw Roger last night?'

Bianca pretended surprise. 'Did I say that? I was thinking of last *week* at the Glenfield Gallery. He was there with that talented little sister of yours, Krystine.'

With a sinking heart, Carrie was sure Bianca meant exactly what she had said. She had been with Roger last night, and probably all the other nights when he'd failed to call. She felt a driving need to know for sure. 'I haven't seen much of Roger since I came here,' she said carefully. 'What has he been doing with himself?'

It was phrased in the manner of a casual enquiry, although she doubted that Bianca was fooled.

Bianca shrugged elaborately. 'Oh, being seen around town. You know what artists are like. They need an audience when they aren't working.'

'Roger told me he *was* working this week,' Carrie said. She knew she was digging her own grave with her teeth but she was unable to stop herself. 'He said he had a backlog of "Emily" strips to catch up on.'

'Then I suppose he was working,' the other woman said lightly. 'But I reminded him about what they say about all work and no play.'

So he had been doing his playing with Bianca. It explained why he hadn't called since Carrie had arrived. She had tried to call him first at the hotel then at the studio at Brooklyn. Both times, the phone had rung and rung unanswered.

Well, at least she now knew where she stood. Foolishly, she had let him beguile her with sweet words and promises until he had got her into his bed, then he had moved on to the next conquest.

How else could she explain his reluctance to visit her here? The memory of how easy she had made it for him brought a glow of shame to Carrie's cheeks. When they had made love, she had really believed he wanted to marry her. With some misgivings, she had accepted his explanation that he was working. Now Bianca was confirming her worst fears.

The other woman rose gracefully. 'I'd best be on my way. Thanks for the rest and the chat. I'll say hello to Roger for you when I see him.'

'When might that be?' Carrie asked huskily.

'I don't really know. Quite possibly tonight.'

Without a backward glance, she whirled out of the dining-room in a blaze of scarlet silk. Minutes later, Carrie heard the throaty roar of a powerful car engine, then it raced off down the circular drive towards the Great Western Highway.

She sat back on her heels, the duster clenched tightly

in her hand. How could she have been such an idiot as to fall for the oldest line in the book? Roger must have had a good laugh at her expense, remembering how readily she had given in to his sweet words.

Then she took a stern grip on herself. What had Bianca actually said—that she and Roger had been together? Now she made herself think clearly, she hadn't actually said anything definite, merely suggesting that she and Roger were on intimate terms. Bianca was relying on Carrie's jealousy to do the rest.

She got to her feet and gathered up the cleaning things. There was only one way to find out what was going on and that was to call Roger and ask him. This time, she would keep trying until she got him on the telephone, no matter how long it took.

When she finally got through, the hotel confirmed that Roger had moved out without making a further reservation. She was left with only the number of the studio at Brooklyn to try. This time, she was rewarded by Roger's velvet tones but before she could say anything, he intoned, 'You have called Gil Marten's Brooklyn studio. Mr Marten is away at present but will be happy to return your call if you leave a message after you hear the tone.'

A high-pitched beep sounded in her ear and she slowly replaced the receiver. Of course, the studio did belong to Gil Marten so most calls would be for him. She could have left a message, she supposed, but she wasn't sure how one used a stranger's answering machine to ask one's fiancé whether he was having an affair with another woman.

She smiled to herself, refreshed by the very idea. She must be overreacting to Bianca's insinuations. It was probably just what Bianca wanted her to do.

Feeling much better, Carrie decided to take a well-deserved break. The dining-room gleamed from her attentions, so she made herself a cup of fragrant herb tea and took it and the morning paper out on to the balcony at the front of the guesthouse.

The black and white marble floor and Italianate columns gave the terrace a cool, inviting air. She sat down at a wrought-iron table and spread the paper in front of her.

Her attention wandered when she tried to concentrate on the articles, so she flipped to the comics page, hardly aware she was doing so until Roger's strip met her eye.

What was Lucy doing now? she wondered curiously.

Lucy herself was not in evidence this morning, but two of Emily's neighbours, gossipy old women, were standing outside Emily's door talking about Harvey, the decorator.

The speech bubbles were closely filled with Roger's neat, hand lettering. 'How she can take up with that Harvey person, I don't know,' said the first. 'Doesn't she know he's really . . .' Then the second neighbour interrupted, saying, 'Hush, someone's coming!'

She closed the paper crossly. Like the rest of Roger's readers, she would have to wait till tomorrow to find out Harvey's dark secret.

Did Roger harbour a secret of his own? she wondered pensively, or was the strip pure fiction as he had insisted all along? She was so accustomed to Lucy's antics paralleling her own that she automatically looked for a hidden message in "Emily" these days. Chiding herself for being fanciful, she drained her teacup and decided to find herself something useful— and distracting—to do. There was no shortage of such activities at Megalong.

Before she could go inside, she heard the crunch of

tyres on gravel and a taxi pulled up alongside the porch. Carrie's smile broadened as she saw who the newcomer was.

'Mum! You're home, how wonderful!'

She hurried to take her mother's case and help her up the steps into the house, although Kay said she could manage perfectly well.

'I'm fine, really,' she insisted. 'Remember, I've spent all of last week at your place doing absolutely nothing!'

'I thought you were spending another week with Krys,' Carrie said.

'I was, but I'm so used to being busy that doing nothing was more worrisome than restful. I kept thinking of all there was to do here.'

'But you knew I'd take care of everything.' Carrie's tone was unwillingly reproachful.

'I know, darling. I didn't mean to sound ungrateful.' She looked around the tiled hall with its gleaming, timber staircase. 'Everything looks lovely. You have been working hard.'

Carrie smiled. 'And wondering how you manage to keep up with everything!'

Her mother shrugged. 'I've often asked myself the same question. You do what you have to, I suppose.'

Happy to have her mother's company and to see her looking so well, Carrie led the way to the small sitting-room off Kay's private apartment. 'You sit down here and I'll fetch you a cup of tea.'

Kay grimaced and held up both hands. 'Please, no more tea. Krys has been force-feeding me with the stuff. Haven't we any wine in the fridge?'

Smiling, Carrie poured two glasses of chilled white wine and placed one on the table beside Kay, then dropped into the chair opposite. 'Good health!' she said sincerely, raising her glass in a toast.

Kay returned the gesture and took a long draught of wine, obviously relishing it. 'Thank you, darling. Now tell me how you've been managing.'

'Not too badly. With the place only half full now, most of the work revolved around the dining-room.'

Kay set her wineglass down. 'You're not unhappy over my decision to sell, are you?'

You're entitled to your happiness,' Carrie said firmly. 'The decision is made. Let's not even discuss it. I'm much more interested in what you plan to do next.'

With fast-beating heart, she waited for Kay's answer, praying that it would be the one she was hoping for.

It was. 'I've decided to go north and look after Oscar, if he'll have me,' Kay confessed, her expression girlishly shy.

'After the way he spoke about you, I think there's no doubt about it,' Carrie assured her.

'Then you think I'm doing the right thing?'

Carrie knelt beside her mother's chair and took her hand. 'Don't ever doubt it. Now that you have no responsibilities, the two of you should be very happy together.'

Excitement flushed Kay's attractive face. 'On the proceeds of Megalong, we should be able to live quite comfortably.' She laughed suddenly. 'Oh, Carrie, imagine me living in a commune!'

Glad to be able to reassure her, Carrie said, 'It isn't a hippy place at all, Mum. It's just kind of . . . rustic . . . but quite charming. Most of the people are younger than Dad, but they're all of like mind. I'm sure you'll fit in beautifully if you give yourself time.'

It was a turnaround for her to be giving her mother advice, she thought ruefully, especially since not so long ago she would have been appalled at what Kay intended to do. Roger had accused Carrie of being a witch, but he was the one who had worked his magic on her attitudes.

Returning to her own seat, she asked, 'How is Krys's exhibition coming along?' Even though other artists much more distinguished than Krys were involved, they had all fallen into the habit of calling it Krys's exhibition.

'Wonderfully. She and Roger have been at the gallery until late every night this week, getting everything ready.'

'Roger has been helping Krys?' she echoed stupidly.

'Of course. He has to work all day on his "Emily" strip, which he tells us might be syndicated in the United States soon. So he's only been available to help Krys in the evenings.'

Carrie could hardly believe her ears. If he had been so busy with work, Roger couldn't possibly have been with Bianca West. Shameful heat spread through her body as she thought of the message she had nearly left for Roger on Gil Marten's answering machine. She was glad now that she had simply hung up.

Kay looked at her anxiously. 'Is something the matter Carrie, you've gone quite pale?'

'No, nothing's the matter, Mum.' Quite the opposite, in fact. Everything was suddenly, gloriously fine again. The only reason Roger hadn't called was because he had been so busy, not because he had lost interest in her.

Kay sat forward. 'You haven't told me how your job hunting is going.'

Some of the elation left Carrie's face. 'Not good, I'm afraid. I haven't been able to make many enquiries from here, but already I can see that it won't be easy to find a job with hours which will dovetail with teacher training.'

She brightened a little. 'However, I have written to a number of colleges about their courses. They tell me I may qualify as a mature student. They give you credit for commercial experience as well as education these days.'

Kay smiled. 'That's wonderful, darling. Have you found out when you'll be able to start?'

Taking a sip of her wine, Carrie frowned. 'First, I have to qualify for entrance. Then I may have to wait until the start of the next college year.'

Kay looked sympathetic. 'What a shame! I know you were hoping to start as soon as possible.'

'Never mind; I'm determined to get there.' She had very little choice. She had burned her bridges behind her now.

'Do you regret leaving your job at Petrie's?' her mother asked, reading her thoughts.

Emphatically, Carrie shook her head. If she hadn't she might not have made her peace with Oscar—or become engaged to Roger. 'No, no regrets,' she confirmed. She recalled Roger's comment that she liked everything cut and dried. 'I'm only worried about what the future holds. I've never been so uncertain about everything as I am now.'

'All of life is uncertain,' Kay reminded her. 'The things we think are so steady and reliable often turn out to be the most nebulous. Sometimes all we can do is go with the tide.'

Going with the tide was easier said than done, Carrie reflected during the following days as she continued to help her mother manage Megalong.

No matter how busy her hands were, her mind kept dwelling on Roger. The memory of their magical two days in Kempsey sent shivers of longing shafting through her. Though it was just over two weeks ago, she felt as if an age had passed since she saw him.

In the distance, the sound of the lion-headed door knocker reverberated through the hall. Kay was upstairs taking the nap Carrie insisted she needed every afternoon, so she straightened from her task of cleaning the black and white tiled terrace. It was probably a salesman of some sort.

But the tall, breathtakingly handsome man who stood on the front porch was no salesman. 'Roger!' she squealed in delight, and threw herself into his arms.

Only then she remembered how dusty and damp she was from her exertions. She tried to pull away but he held her tightly. 'Where do you think you're going? It's only been a week and I feel like a drowning man who's just been thrown a rope.'

'But I'm filthy!' she protested.

He held her at arm's length but still in the same firm grip. 'To me, you're the most beautiful sight in these mountains.'

At her urging, he followed her inside and waited while she washed off some of the grime and tugged a comb through her hair. By the time she emerged, feeling at least presentable, she had remembered how annoyed she had been with him not so long before.

He sensed the change in her mood as soon as she joined him in the family sitting-room. 'What happened to the warm welcome?'

'What happened to being in touch?' she echoed coolly, trying not to be distracted by the sight of him, so tanned and lithe, leaning nonchalantly against the mantelpiece.

He looked puzzled. 'I'm here, aren't I? Surely a personal visit is better than a phone call?'

She sighed in exasperation. Would their whole

married life be like this—a see-saw of anxious waiting followed by joyous reunions? 'It's been over a week,' she pointed out.

He folded his arms. 'I see. So I'm in the doghouse again. Well, I suppose it's better if you tell me instead of bottling it up and expecting me to read your mind. I suppose it's no use saying I've been working.'

'I know you have,' she said matter-of-factly, 'Mum told me. She said you were working on "Emily" all day and helping Krys with the exhibition in the evenings. When did you think you'd find time to paint a wall mural for Bianca West?' She hadn't meant to say that. It was out before she stopped to think.

He looked thoughtful. 'Has Miss West been making mischief again?'

He hadn't answered her question, she noticed pointedly. 'She came here,' she said levelly. 'She was worried that all work and no play was making you a dull boy.'

'Implying that I was playing with her,' he concluded. 'All I did was agree to think about her mural, hoping she'd forget all about it in time. For God's sake, Carrie, predatory women aren't my style, you should know that.'

She did, but was relieved when he confirmed it. 'All the same, Bianca is wealthy enough to keep you in comfort while you work,' she said thoughtfully.

He looked annoyed. 'Which would be wonderful if I was looking for a meal ticket—which I'm not.'

He crossed the floor in purposeful strides and pulled her into his arms. 'The only comfort I can take from this nonsense is that if you're so jealous of Bianca for no good reason, you must really care for me.'

Wide-eyed, she looked up at him, feeling her body

respond vibrantly as it always did to his nearness. 'Can you doubt it?'

For answer, he cupped the back of her head in his hand and tilted her head up so he could kiss her with fierce possessiveness. Heat flooded through her loins and she instinctively pressed closer against him. When her lips parted under his and their tongues touched, jets of fire tore along her veins.

'God I've missed you,' he breathed, his lips moving against her mouth. 'When can we be married?'

'Soon, my darling. Whenever you like.'

He lifted his head and gazed adoringly into her eyes. 'Tomorrow.'

Laughing, she freed herself and went to the window. 'We can't do that. It wouldn't be fair to Krys.'

'Damn Krys and the whole world. I want you in my life . . . in my bed,' he added, his voice deepening. 'One of the reasons I've been working like a demon is to keep my mind off you. It's the cartoonist's equivalent of the cold shower.'

The idea thrilled and touched her, even while it frightened her to be placed on such a pedestal. What if she disappointed him? 'You make me sound like some sort of sex goddess,' she said uneasily.

His gaze intensified and he followed her to the window. 'You are, to me. I'm an all-or-nothing man, Carrie. And you're my all.'

She turned to find herself trapped in his arms. 'All right, then,' she conceded, 'we can be married in two weeks. The last of Mum's guests will have left then. They've all been given notice that Megalong is being sold, and we aren't taking any new bookings.'

He groaned aloud. 'Here am I panting with desire, and you're being so darned practical.'

It was exactly what she intended to be. If Kay had

taken a firmer hand with Oscar, their lives might have been very different. 'One of us has to think of these things,' she said primly.

He laughed suddenly. 'I can see you're going to be a great stabilising influence on this poor artist's life.'

His tone wounded her. He sounded as if he was mocking her again, when she was in deadly earnest. She turned her head away.

Seeing her hurt expression, he stopped laughing. 'Hey, don't take it so much to heart! I know you only have my best interests in mind.'

'Our best interests,' she amended.

'All right, *our* best interests. Have you thought you could be worrying needlessly? My "Emily" strip brings in some income you know, and there's a chance it may be syndicated in the United States.'

How often had she heard Oscar chasing such rainbows? When she was a child, there was always a big contract in the offing, or some other windfall 'just around the corner'. Couldn't Roger see that relying on such things was foolhardy? Fortunately, she didn't intend to leave it all to him. Once she was qualified to teach, they could live on her regular income. Roger's commissions would be the icing on the cake instead of, as Oscar had tried to make it, the cake itself.

'You don't have much faith in me, do you?' Roger asked as he watched the changing expressions on her face.

She hastened to reassure him. 'Of course I do. It's the cartoon market I refuse to trust.'

'Well as long as that's all it is. I'd hate to think you didn't trust me to look after you.'

'The days when a man had to "look after" a woman all her life are long gone!' she said in exasperation. 'You said you aren't looking for a meal ticket—well, neither am I!'

For some reason, he seemed hugely pleased with her outburst. She faced him with hands on hips. 'Now what are you laughing at?'

He became grave, although the sparkle remained in his startling blue eyes. 'I'm not laughing, honestly. I'm just looking forward to the surprise I've planned for you next week.'

Instantly, she was diverted. 'What surprise?'

He spread his hands. 'No clues now, you'll have to wait until after the opening when I'll let you in on a secret.'

'You've sold "Emily" to America,' she hazarded.

'Nope. And stop fishing. You'll find out on Monday night.'

'You sound like Harvey, with his deep dark secret. What is it by the way?'

He chuckled. 'At least you're still a fan. Don't worry, it will all be resolved in the end—which, incidentally, is the end of next week for this story.'

So he wasn't going to give any secrets away, either his own or Harvey's. Harvey, she had already concluded, would turn out to be someone rich and successful in disguise, so that Lucy would be even happier if she decided to marry him. But what could Roger be hiding? Carrie was sure it had something to do with his work.

Despite his evasiveness, she felt sure he was on the verge of selling his cartoon strip to an American newspaper. He was probably waiting until the deal was signed and sealed to tell her. She smiled at him. 'Have it your own way. Lucy is bound to tell me, even if you don't.'

'You still see yourself as Lucy, don't you?' he said good-humouredly. 'Well I'm afraid you're in for a disappointment this time. Lucy doesn't know my secret and neither will you, my girl, until Monday.' He looked around. 'How is your mother?'

By now, she knew him well enough to know when she would get nothing more out of him. As one who liked all her i's dotted and her t's crossed, she felt frustrated, but there was nothing she could do about it until he chose to tell her. She sighed impotently. 'Mum's fine. She's upstairs, resting. I try to make sure she takes a nap each afternoon, although she says the idleness is driving her crazy.'

'Tell her I called and give her my regards,' he said, moving towards the door.

A flash of disappointment lanced through her. 'You're leaving already? But you've only just got here.'

He looked apologetic. 'I wish I could stay longer, but I stole this time away from work as it is.' He touched her under the chin. 'Maybe it's better this way. If I stay here much longer, I know I'm going to make passionate love to you.'

If he stayed much longer, she would let him, she acknowledged. Having him in the same room was enough to arouse her to fever pitch. She ached for his possession in a way which would have astonished her a few weeks ago. 'You're probably right,' she agreed. 'I'll see you on Monday at the opening.'

'Yes, but not for long,' he warned her. 'I'll be up to my ears with reporters and whatnot.'

She frowned. 'Surely you won't be as involved as all that? It's not as if your work is on exhibition, after all.'

He seemed about to say something, then checked himself. 'You're right, of course. But I promised Krys I would help her to handle the press.'

'I see. What about after the opening?'

'I'm all yours.' He thought for a moment. 'In case I get tied up, wait for me in the wine bar alongside the gallery. it has its own entrance, or you can go in from the gift shop attached to the gallery. We'll have dinner together.'

'What about Mum? I'm drivng her down with me on Monday night, then she'll be staying with Krys for a few days while I come back to take care of things here. Most of the guests will be gone by then, but someone has to be here for the estate agent who's handling the sale.'

'Then I'll ask Krys if she'll drive your mother back to your flat after the opening.' He stifled a groan. 'Your mother is a charming woman, but by Monday I'll be in no shape to share you with anyone.'

She knew exactly how he felt. The ache in her own body was equally strong, needing only his touch to inflame it into active desire. 'I know,' she agreed, her voice barely a whisper, 'I feel the same way.'

He lifted her hand and touched it to his lips in a courtly gesture. 'Until Monday, then.'

Over the hand he still held captive, their eyes met and she inclined her head imperceptibly. 'Until Monday.'

By unspoken agreement, he found his own way out, leaving her standing in the sitting-room, her whole being vibrating with longing for him. Monday was only a few short days away but it felt like an eternity.

She wrapped her arms around her body in pale imitation of his embrace. It was the sweetest torment not seeing him until the opening. She was also consumed with curiosity. What secret was he going to reveal to her when they met?

CHAPTER TEN

THE Glenfield Gallery was already thronged with people when Carrie and her mother arrived on Monday night after driving down from the mountains that afternoon.

Carrie pulled up at the main entrance of the Regency brick building. 'You go inside. I'll be ages finding somewhere to park.'

Her mother nodded agreement and started to unbuckle her seat-belt. 'In case we get separated, have a lovely time with Roger tonight, darling.'

Carrie had explained about their date. 'Are you sure you don't mind going home with Krys?' she asked again.

'Of course not. You wouldn't want me tagging along, playing gooseberry, now would you?'

Carrie grinned. 'You make it sound as though we might get up to something.'

Kay leaned towards her conspiratorially. 'Know something? I hope you do. He's a fine young man and I can't wait to have him for a son-in-law.'

'Are all mothers as broad-minded as you?' Carrie laughed.

Kay winked at her. 'Much more than our daughters give us credit for.'

All the same, Carrie felt sure most mothers were not as understanding as Kay, even in this enlightened day and age. She counted her blessings, thankful that Kempsey was close enough so they could keep in touch after Kay went to live with Oscar.

Fleetingly she envisaged a small boy, a carbon-copy of Roger, running around the compound at Koompartoo and smiled to herself. Much as she yearned to have Roger's children, she wanted the two of them to be secure first. Her memories of her own childhood deprivations were too vivid to want to inflict them on her own children.

With an effort she concentrated on finding a parking space. She and Roger weren't even married and already she was imagining herself as the mother of his children. What would he say if he knew?

Finally, she found a tiny space between two Mercedes and manoeuvred her Escort in between them. There goes the neighbourhood, she thought wryly, comparing her modest car with its gleaming companions. They must belong to guests at the opening, she surmised.

A look at the crowd inside the gallery confirmed her guess. Most of the men wore black tie, making her glad that she and her mother had dressed with care. She felt quite confident in her black jersey cocktail dress with its matching jacket.

Her mother was already engrossed in conversation with an elderly man whom Carrie recognised as a former guest at Megalong, so she waved to them and plunged into the throng.

There was as yet no sign of Roger but she soon located Krys who looked stunning in a jade jumpsuit trimmed with sequins across one shoulder.

She flung herself at Carrie on sight. 'You made it! How's Mum?'

'Fantastic. She's already found herself a beau so I came looking for you.' She glanced around. 'Well, you wanted a crowd. It sure looks like you got your wish!'

Krys looked pleased but self-deprecating. 'Most of

them are here because of Gil Marten, not me. I can hardly believe my humble efforts are hanging alongside his. Pinch me, just to make sure I'm awake.'

Laughing, Carrie shook her head. 'There's no need. It's true, I promise you.' Then Krys was dragged away to answer some questions, so Carrie accepted a catalogue from an attendant and studied it eagerly.

Starting from the entrance, she worked her way around all the pictures until she had inspected every one of her sister's drawings. She was glowing with pride in Krys by the time she completed the circuit, and was so engrossed in her perusal that she cannoned into a woman doing the same thing.

'I'm sorry. Why—Helen!' she exclaimed.

Her former boss smiled back. 'Carrie, it *is* you! I suppose you're here to support your sister on her big night.'

Carrie nodded. 'She's worked so hard for this success. She deserves it.'

'I agree. You see, I'm a bit of a collector of black and white line work. I even have one of Norman Lindsay's old political cartoons. And I think Krystine Doyle has great promise.'

A waiter offered them champagne and they sipped it in companionable silence for a few minutes until Helen said nervously, 'I don't suppose you'd consider coming back to Petrie's?'

'You mean to work with you?'

'In the book department. I'm sorry for what happened, Carrie. I had a splitting migraine that day or I wouldn't have been so harsh with you.'

Carrie watched the bubbles rise in her glass before she answered. 'I'm sorry too, Helen. I don't know what possessed me to let you think I was ill when I wasn't.'

Helen smiled warmly. 'Well, I do. Love makes fools

of us all sometimes. But I meant what I said—the job is yours if you want it. I've given up hope of finding a replacement half as good as you.'

The warm glow of Helen's praise was dampened by Carrie's need to disappoint her. 'I'm sorry, but I can't come back. I've decided to fulfil a dream of mine and try to qualify as a teacher, so I'll only be able to work at whatever fits in with my course.'

'Then why not come back as a casual? We could work out the hours as soon as you know when you're available.'

'I could work full time until the start of the new college year,' Carrie offered, feeling excitement well up inside her. 'As long as you wouldn't mind when I had to switch to part time.'

Helen raised her glass in salute. 'Then it's settled. Come and see me as soon as you're ready and we'll work out the details.'

It was too good to be true, Carrie thought as Helen moved off to greet someone else she knew. Although she had barely acknowledged it to herself, the thought of being unemployed had scared Carrie. Now she would have some security when she and Roger were married.

'You look very pleased with yourself.' Carrie looked up as Bianca West approached her. Even the sight of the society belle, chic in a multi-coloured dress by a famous designer couldn't dampen Carrie's buoyant mood.

'Hello, Bianca. It's a wonderful party, isn't it?' Let her guess why Carrie was so happy tonight. By tomorrow, it would be public knowledge.

Bianca shrugged. 'They're much of a muchness. I've bought one of your little sister's efforts, in case you're interested.'

Astonished, Carrie stared at her. 'Why would you do that?' It wasn't like Bianca to be philanthropic unless there was something in it for her.

The other woman's gaze was shrewd. 'I have a hunch she's going to go far so her early work will be valuable one day, mark my words.'

Hearing Bianca speak of Krys as someone who might one day be famous, Carrie felt a twinge of guilt. She was suddenly glad that her sister had been strong enough to override her disapproval.

Bianca suddenly drew herself up, her long lashes fluttering. Even without Bianca's reaction, Carrie knew Roger had entered the gallery from the way her nerve endings suddenly prickled. She drew a breath as their eyes met. How handsome he looked in his dress suit, the frilled shirt dazzlingly white in contrast to the inky black of his suit and tie!

He smiled when he saw her. 'Hello, darling. Enjoying yourself? Oh, hello, Bianca.'

Although he was looking at Carrie, Bianca appropriated his tender greeting without a qualm. 'It wasn't much of a do until you arrived,' she purred. 'I wanted to talk to you about that wall mural of mine. I saw the one you did at Katoomba and it was wonderful.'

Roger had eyes only for Carrie, and she read warm approval in their blue depths as he took in the low-cut dress with its softly draped jacket. 'Mural?' he said distractedly, then remembered. 'Oh, yes. But that was a one-off as a return favour. I won't have time to do it for you myself, but I can recommend someone,' he offered blandly.

The temperature dropped appreciably. 'Don't trouble yourself,' Bianca murmured frostily and moved off into the crowd, sweeping a glass of champagne off a waiter's tray as she went.

'I don't think you're her Mr Wonderful any more,' Carrie giggled, sipping her own champagne. 'She bought one of Krys's pictures, so you could at least be nice to her.'

He grimaced. 'First you're unhappy because I pay her attention, then you complain because I don't jump when she snaps her fingers.'

Carrie touched his arm. 'I suppose I feel more generous towards her now I know you don't fancy her.'

His expression grew teasing. 'What makes you think I don't fancy her.'

'Because you fancy me, and three's a crowd,' Carrie said decisively. She began to tell Roger about Helen's job offer but was interrupted when Krys came hurrying up to them.

'The press have arrived, Roger. They all want pictures and interviews. What do I do now?'

He looked apologetically at Carrie. 'I warned you this could happen. Relax, Krys, they don't bite. I'll come and rescue you.'

Suppressing the merest twinge of jealousy, Carrie forced a smile as the two of them headed towards Krys's display. She would have a lifetime with Roger. She was big enough to share him with Krys for just an evening.

After standing alone for a few minutes, she sought out her mother who was resting on a chair near the entrance. 'Do you feel all right?' she asked in concern.

Kay nodded. 'I'm fine, darling. I was just getting my breath back. I didn't expect to run into so many people I knew.'

'I'm glad you're having fun. Can I get you a drink or anything?'

'No, dear, I'm being looked after, so you go and enjoy yourself. I expect you want to admire Roger's work.'

'I didn't know any of this was his,' Carrie said, baffled. Why hadn't Roger said some of his pictures were on show? 'I saw all of Krys's and Oscar's work, but . . .'

They were interrupted as a portly gentleman in a too-tight dinner suit sailed towards Kay with two glasses of champagne. 'Ah, there you are, my dear. I hope I wasn't gone too long.'

'Of course not. Colonel Dougherty, this is my other daughter, Caroline.'

Carrie murmured a greeting then left them talking. She made another complete circuit of the gallery, looking closely at the signatures this time, but she still couldn't find any of Roger's drawings. Her mother must have meant another gallery or exhibition. The room was becoming hot and stuffy, and she remembered Roger's arrangement to meet her in the wine bar after the opening. The affair was due to end in half an hour or so, although she doubted whether it would, but Roger would probably have had enough by then, too.

With difficulty, she made her way through the crowd to the gift shop she had noticed adjacent to the gallery. According to Roger, the wine bar was just beyond it.

The gift shop was open and Carrie paused on her way through, to browse among the displays.

The shop sold all kinds of arty gifts, from drawing sets and cut-out books for children, to adult painting sets and prints of gallery exhibits. There was also a display of art-related books and Carrie was drawn to this at once.

Reflexively, she began to tidy the display, then remembered that it wasn't her job and let her hand drop.

Then one of the volumes caught her eye and she reached for it. It was a glossy coffee-table book comprising reproductions of the best of Gil Marten's work. What a wonderful gift it would make for Krys! With any luck, Carrie could even get it autographed. Excitedly, she carried the book to the counter where a bored-looking young woman was examining her finger-nails. 'How much is this please?'

The woman told her the price and Carrie reached for her purse. 'I'll take it.'

'Would you like it gift-wrapped?'

'No, thank you.' Family pride prompted her to add, 'I'm hoping Mr Marten will autograph it as a gift for my sister—she's Krystine Doyle, whose work is on show tonight.'

The woman brightened a little. 'Then she'll like the book, I'm sure.'

'You haven't seen Mr Marten tonight, have you?' Carrie asked. Surely someone who worked in an art gallery would at least know what he looked like.

'I'm not likely to, dear.' She crooked a finger at Carrie, urging her to come closer. 'You see, he doesn't exist.'

It was such a ridiculous comment that Carrie almost laughed aloud, until she realised that the woman was serious. 'But I've been to his studio, and all his work is on show here,' she said.

The saleswoman laughed. 'I don't doubt it. What I mean is, Gil Marten is a pen-name—or whatever the artist's equivalent might be. It isn't common knowledge and I'm probably not supposed to know, but I saw some of the paperwork when his pictures came in for the showing. His full name is Roger Gilmarten Torkan—you know, the cartoonist.'

She certainly did know! Somehow, she paid for her purchase and carried it out of the shop and into the next-door wine bar, where she sank on to a seat in a

secluded booth. What a fool she had been not to make
the connection herself! Roger had said that Gil Marten
was a sort of relative. She just hadn't worked out how
closely they were related.

It all made sense now—his cavalier attitude to
money, and the way he had made himself at home in
the Brooklyn house. The hotel she thought he lived in
must have been for convenience while he was making
personal appearances in Sydney. She cringed as she
recalled the way he had mocked her when she offered to
keep them both while he drew his cartoons.

She was dimly aware of a waiter approaching and
bringing the glass of mineral water she requested, but
everything else moved around her in a blur, unseen. All
she could think was that Roger had played a cruel joke
on her and she didn't understand why.

Krys must have known, so must her mother—which
explained why she'd asked if Carrie had seen Roger's
work in the gallery tonight. Did everyone know but
her? Why hadn't they said something, to prevent her
making such a colossal fool of herself?

'Ah, there you are. Have you been waiting long?'

All day she had looked forward to the moment when
she would have him to herself but as she met his
caressing gaze she felt more alone than ever. 'Hello,
Roger,' she said flatly. 'Or should I say, Mr Marten?'

His tender expression turned into one of annoyance.
'How did you find out?'

'Sooner or later, someone was bound to let it slip,
since I was one of the few people who didn't know,' she
said coldly.

He exhaled slowly. 'Damn! I swore Krys and your
mother to secrecy until I could tell you myself tonight.
How long have you known?'

'Does it matter?' She was more anxious as to *why* he

had deceived her, and all he cared about was when his lie had been discovered.

A shadow darkened his even features and the blue eyes grew increasingly cold. 'Yes, it does matter. It means the difference between whether you love me for myself, or for what I could give you.' When she didn't reply, he mistook her stunned silence for self-condemnation. 'I might have guessed it was Gil Marten you were in love with, not me, from the way you went on and on about meeting him. You know, you really had me duped with your martyr act and all that noble stuff about getting a job to support both of us.'

Her throat was too choked to form words, far less contradict him. Why was he being so cruel? He was the one who had deceived her, yet he made it sound as if she was the one in the wrong.

Her tears threatened to spill over right here in the wine bar. Well, she was damned if she would give him that satisfaction. Blindly she got to her feet. 'Think what you like,' she flung at him as she groped her way out.

How she managed the drive back to Megalong, she never knew. Luckily, she'd only drunk two half glasses of champagne so she was fit to drive, at least legally, although her emotions were in such turmoil that it was all she could do to manage the car on the mountainous roads.

Roger's behaviour made no sense. Why had he allowed her to go on and on about being the breadwinner, so he could carry on as a cartoonist? He could have saved her from her own stupidity by simply admitting that he was better known under a pen-name.

By the time she reached Megalong, two hours later, she was much calmer, although she felt as if she had left part of herself behind at the Glenfield Gallery.

When she let herself into her mother's apartment she realised she was still clutching the Gil Marten book she had purchased for Krys.

As if hypnotised, she began to turn the glossy pages. The book was a collection of his famous wildlife studies, sketched in South America.

Now she knew why he had been travelling down the wild rivers of New Guinea. It wasn't because he was a foolhardy adventurer as she'd first thought. It was to gather material for his meticulously detailed sketches. No wonder he had been so evasive about his travels! Explaining what he was doing would have given away his other identity. It seemed she had been horribly wrong about him on all counts.

All except one. She loved him. She wasn't wrong about that. Even now, holding his book in her hands was like holding the man himself, and she felt the familiar warmth stirring inside her. She turned to the back of the book, searching for the author's biography. This time, there was no photo, since Gil Marten preferred to keep his identity secret. But there was a brief note about the man.

Knowing his secret, she readily recognised Roger in the brief description, especially the parts about his love of adventure and his willingness to risk personal danger to capture the sketches he wanted.

Tearfully, she hugged the book to her chest. Where was its author now? Was he thinking she had only agreed to marry him because she knew who he really was? Or was he consoling himself with Bianca West's flamboyant company? The heiress would be only too happy to accommodate him, Carrie was sure.

Somehow, she knew he wasn't with Bianca. 'I'm an all-or-nothing man,' he had said, and she had the feeling he had meant it. It evidently applied to his relationships as well. By admitting that she knew who he really was, Carrie had forfeited the all and ended up with nothing.

Why hadn't she simply told him how she'd found out about Gil Marten? He would have known then that it had nothing to do with why she loved him. She possessed the same streak of stubbornness as her mother, she acknowledged painfully. She could no more bring herself to beg for his understanding, than he could for hers if the roles were reversed.

The telephone shrilled and she froze, wondering wildly if it was Roger. She was tempted to let it ring until common sense told her it could be a business call connected with Megalong. Her mother had entrusted her with the running of the place so she had to find out who was calling.

Reluctantly, she lifted the receiver and the long-distance pips beeped in her ear. 'Hello?' she said over them.

'Carrie, is that you?'

The tension drained out of her in a rush. 'Oh, hi, Krys. I thought you'd be out on the town celebrating by now.'

'Too tired,' her sister said, in heartfelt tones. 'After talking to all those reporters and posing for pictures, I'm exhausted.'

'But it went well,' Carrie assured her. 'I'm proud of you, little sister.'

There was a choked silence, then Krys said, 'Thanks. I know you didn't want me to try my wings, but I'm glad I didn't disappoint you when I insisted.'

'Of course you didn't. Don't be silly. I'm as proud of you as I can be.'

'Thanks again.' There was a pause. 'It isn't why I called though. I saw Roger on his own after the evening ended. I thought you two had a date.'

Unwilling to open the floodgates by talking about it, Carrie said flatly, 'We did. It didn't work out.'

'But you're still engaged?'

It was a question she hadn't dared to consider yet. 'I don't know. Look, Krys, it was a long drive back and I'm tired too . . .'

She could picture her sister making a gesture of protest. 'OK, I get the message. Butt out, little sister.'

'Don't be an idiot,' said Carrie fondly. 'Your advice is always welcome, you know that. These days your track record at being right is a lot better than mine. The only thing is . . .'

'Yes?'

'Why didn't you tell me that Roger Torkan was also Gil Marten?'

Krys drew a sharp breath. 'Is that what you two quarrelled about? Gee, Carrie, I only kept it to myself because Roger was so insistent. If I'd known you would be upset about it, I would have told you.'

'It's all right,' Carrie reassured her, regretting the distress she had provoked in her sister's voice. 'What I don't understand is *why* he wanted to keep it from me.'

There was another long silence. 'My guess is, he knew how you felt about cartoonists in general—after Dad I mean—and he wanted to prove you were wrong.'

'But surely, telling me would have done that? He's successful enough to convince anybody.'

'That's just the point,' Krys said patiently. 'He's successful but at the wrong thing. His wildlife pictures are . . .' She struggled for a word. 'They're respectable. The sort of thing a mother doesn't mind telling people her son does for a living. At least, his mother does.'

Light was beginning to dawn. 'He thought I, of all people, would accept him as a cartoonist first and last.'

'Uh-huh. From the way he tells it, Roger has been fighting this kind of prejudice all his life. He's earned the right to be proud of what he does. It's understandable that he prefers to be known for his cartoons, rather than his animal studies, even though they earn him a lot more money and prestige.'

'I blew it again, didn't I?' Carrie said miserably.

''Fraid so, big sister. There's only one thing left for you to do.'

Shoot myself, Carrie thought not entirely in jest. Aloud she said, 'What's that?'

'Find Roger and tell him how wrong you've been. If he's the man I think he is, he'll be willing to start afresh but without any silly deception between you this time.'

'You could be right,' Carrie said slowly. They said their goodnights and she hung up. Krys made it sound so easy but she didn't know Roger as well as Carrie did—or thought she did until tonight. He was the all-or-nothing man, remember? Since he now thought she hadn't given him her trust willingly, would he accept it on any other terms?

Her head ached with trying to make sense of it all, so she got undressed and ready for bed. As she slid in between the cold sheets of her mother's double bed, she looked longingly at the empty half. She had never felt more alone in her life.

The last guests were due to leave Megalong next morning. As well, there was the bookkeeping to be brought up to date and the newly vacated rooms to clean, so she had no time to brood on her problems.

Her mother had decided to put Megalong up for auction, and the estate agent had advertised the property. With the chance that prospective buyers might drop in at short notice to inspect the house, it had to be looking its best all the time. As it turned out, three people came to look at the house during the day, so Carrie had plenty of distractions for which she was thankful. She couldn't have borne too much time to think just now. Her emotions felt numb, but the floodgates had to open soon and she would feel the full impact of all she had lost.

The interruptions from the estate agent kept her alert and busy. No sooner did she scrub the tiled hall floor clean of footprints than a new group of people arrived to track across it again.

It was mid-week before she had any time to herself. By then, she had alsmost convinced herself that she would get over Roger in time. If only she could make her errant body erase the memory of his caresses, and her mind forget his whispered words of love in the darkness at Kempsey.

She clucked her tongue impatiently. This was useless. She daren't sit and brood because when she did, she remembered what a fool she was. She had driven him away with her lack of faith. Considering his experiences, she could no longer blame him for wanting to keep his alter ego a secret from her.

The morning paper was on the kitchen table and she picked it up, flipping through the pages disinterestedly while she sipped her morning tea.

Unwillingly, she was drawn to the comics page, although she knew that if Lucy had also lost Harvey, she didn't want to know about it.

Still, she was curious about Lucy's progress in the three days since she'd last read 'The Many Loves of Emily'. Maybe Lucy had taken up with another man by now.

Fat chance! she thought mutinously as she looked for the strip.

Although the cartoon was named after her, Emily

herself seldom made an appearance. She was the glue
that held the other characters together. Today, however, Roger had drawn her sitting beside Lucy on a
couch, with her arm around the younger woman.

Emily's speech bubble said, 'Why did he do it?'

Lucy, in tears, was saying, 'If only I'd believed in
him.'

Why did he do what? 'What have you done with
Harvey?' Carrie screamed silently at the page. Surely
poor Harvey hadn't done away with himself because of
unrequited love?

Anxiously, she looked for the preceding day's papers,
but she must have thrown them away. She could get a
copy from the newsagent but it would take too long for
the papers to be delivered. She simply had to know
what Roger had done to Harvey.

Suddenly, her blood chilled, and she stood stock still
in the centre of the kitchen. If Harvey and Lucy were
Roger's depictions of himself and Carrie, Roger could
be telling her that he would kill himself if they couldn't
resolve their differences.

'Oh, my God, no!' It seemed crazy yet all too
possible, especially when she considered Lucy saying if
only she'd believed in Harvey. It was probably the way
Roger felt about Carrie right now.

Panic seized her. What if Roger was going to do
something terrible because of her? She had to find out.

Her fingers shook when she telephoned the estate
agent and explained that she had to leave Megalong for
a few hours. Fortunately, the agent possessed a key so
he could still show customers around. In fact he seemed
happy to have Carrie out of his hair. 'I'll let you know
when I get back,' she promised as she rang off.

Her next call was to the Glenfield Gallery, the most
likely place to start looking for Roger. She was told he

had driven back to his studio after Krys's opening. He was in a foul temper, too, the gallery owner volunteered.

Her heart sank. His studio was hours away but she had no choice but to drive to Brooklyn. Even telephoning him wouldn't fully set her mind at rest. She needed to see for herself that he was safe and well, even if he thought she was crazy. His well-being was all that mattered to her now.

It took her only minutes to change into a tidy pair of denim jeans and a silk shirt; then she grabbed a jacket and her car keys and flew on wings of fear down to her car. She might be reading too much into a comic strip, but she wouldn't rest until she found out for sure.

The village was dark and tranquil when she finally reached it in the early evening. Her stomach rumbled and her head ached from concentrating on the driving. But she clung to her objective, to find Roger before he did anything stupid.

Gil Marten's studio—Roger's studio—she corrected herself—was shrouded in darkness when she pulled up outside. Surely there should be some lights showing if he was here? Her stomach muscles contracted in fear for him.

Cautiously she went inside, finding her way to the living-room by memory. The living-room was palely lit by moonlight and her heart turned over as she took in the scene before her.

Roger was dimly outlined against the night sky. He was standing on a chair in the middle of the room and there was the unmistakable silhouette of a cord around his neck.

'Roger, don't!' she screamed, feeling the blood rush to her head. As he turned towards her, the floor tilted crazily and she collapsed in a heap.

'Carrie, can you hear me? Wake up!'

She came to on a couch and winced as a bright light dazzled her, then she struggled to sit up, remembering the sight that had greeted her. 'Roger, you're all right?'

'Of course I am, but I'm not so sure about you.'

She still felt woozy and leaned back against his supporting arm. 'Thank God, I got here in time.'

'You aren't making sense, darling,' he said gently. 'In time for what?'

'To stop you from killing yourself.'

'Repairing a light fitting isn't usually fatal—unless you forget to turn the power off, which I've already done,' he told her. 'I've just turned it back on.'

She stared at him blankly. 'Repairing a light fitting? Is that what you were doing?' Hysterical laughter bubbled up inside her. 'I thought ... oh, Roger, I thought you were trying to kill yourself!'

His gaze was oddly intense. 'How did you get that idea?'

The words came rushing out, fuelled by hunger, exhaustion and nervous strain. 'I read "Emily" today. I thought Harvey had killed himself because Lucy didn't believe in him.' When Roger said nothing, she went on, 'I thought it was your way of telling me you intended to end it all because I didn't love you for yourself.'

His eyes slid away from hers. 'It worked, didn't it?'

'You mean, you *were* going to kill yourself over me?'

'Nothing quite so dramatic—and I'm truly sorry for giving you a fright just now—but I was getting desperate. I just didn't seem to be able to get through to you any other way than through "Emily".'

Suddenly shy, she ducked her head. 'You're getting through now.'

'Am I? Am I really? I hope so, Carrie, because my

editor is getting sick of rearranging his schedules to suit my love life.'

'You mean you made him put all those strips in just to get through to me?'

He nodded, suddenly grave. 'I might have used a funny medium, but the message is very serious. I love you, Carrie. I can't bear the thought of losing you.'

'Oh, Roger, it took poor old Harvey to make me see that I feel the same about you. I've been such a fool.'

'It depends on whether you decide to stay or walk out of here now,' he said carefully.

She wasn't that much of a fool. 'You mean you'd still want me after all the dumb things I said about you and Gil Marten?' she said shakily. 'Gil Marten might be up there in his ivory tower, but what you do is so much more important. You make people happy, teach them a thing or two . . . you even taught me a few things, like what's important to me.'

He looked uncomfortable. 'Maybe I'm the fool for not trusting you in the first place. Krys and your mother told me you were in love with me long before you found out about my alter ego.'

She nodded, feeling the tears prick the backs of her eyes. 'I only found out who Gil Marten was half an hour before you met me in the wine bar.'

'Why didn't you tell me so then?'

'I was too hurt that you thought me so mercenary you needed to keep it from me. Krys told me why you did it.'

'Krys is a perceptive little lady,' he said. 'I'm going to like having her for a sister-in-law.'

'Not half as mauch as I'll like having you for my husband,' she vouchsafed. 'Oh, Roger, I love you so much—you, the crazy hot-headed cartoonist. I don't care what else you call yourself or what you do for a living as long as you love me back.'

With a groan, he pulled her against him and her mouth opened to his. His mounting passion was mirrored in her quivering responses and the touch of his tongue to hers was so provocative she thought she would explode with desire for him.

Slowly he raised his head. 'I hope you meant what you just said literally, my darling, because I'm not sick this time—unless you count lovesick!'

For answer she pulled his head down again and as one, they moved towards the master bedroom. Lovesickness she could definitely cure.

Much later, as she lay with her head pillowed on his chest, she remembered to say, 'You still haven't told me what Harvey's deep dark secret was. Is he secretly famous too?'

His hand rested on the soft cushion of her breast and he massaged it tenderly, eliciting a groan of response. 'Would you believe me if I tell you I don't know?' he confessed. 'I'm still working on that part of the story.'

She lifted herself until she lay across him, looking curiously into his eyes. 'I thought you cartoonists were supposed to know how your stories come out!'

As he pulled her down so he could capture her mouth, he whispered, 'Only this one, my darling, only this one.'

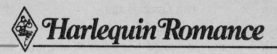
◈ Harlequin Romance

Coming Next Month

2863 BRIDE ON APPROVAL Elizabeth Ashton
Sancia desperately wants to be free from her restrictive upbringing, yet she can't bring herself to escape by way of an arranged marriage—not even to the charming Italian count chosen for her!

2864 THE GOOD-TIME GUY Rosemary Badger
Her boss's relentless pursuit causes problems for office manager Sarah Ames. She's come to Brisbane with her sights fixed on a career and has no time for a man only interested in playing games!

2865 IMPULSIVE ATTRACTION Diana Hamilton
During their first magical meeting in the moonlit woods, it doesn't seem to matter that he's a mysterious itinerant sculptor, while she's a respectable bank manager. But by daylight, the differences between them threaten to destroy their love.

2866 SLEEPING TIGER Joanna Mansell
There's nothing sensible about social butterfly Lady Sophia's suddenly inspired decision to follow a teacher to the Sahara so she can do some worthwhile work with him there. It certainly changes her life—but not quite in the way she expects....

2867 EXCLUSIVE CONTRACT Dixie McKeone
Against all the professional counseling rules about not getting romantically involved with a client, Janet Talbot enthusiastically sets out to rescue an unusually charming housebreaker from a life of crime!

2868 AN OLD AFFAIR Alexandra Scott
Only her father's urgent need for money sends Arabella seeking help from the man she had loved and mysteriously lost seven years ago. His price for giving it is high—one Arabella isn't sure she wants to pay.

Available in October wherever paperback books are sold, or through Harlequin Reader Service.

In the U.S.
901 Fuhrmann Blvd.
P.O. Box 1397
Buffalo, N.Y. 14240-1397

In Canada
P.O. Box 603
Fort Erie, Ontario
L2A 5X3

**For the millions who can't read
Give the Gift of Literacy**

One out of five adults in North America
cannot read or write well enough
to fill out a job application
or understand the directions on a bottle of medicine.

**You can change all this by joining the fight
against illiteracy.**

For more information write to:
Contact, Box 81826, Lincoln, Neb. 68501
In the United States, call toll free: 1-800-228-8813

**The only degree you need
is a degree of caring**

LIT-A-1R

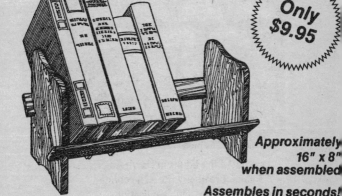

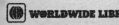

Sarah

MAURA SEGER

Sarah wanted desperately to escape the clutches of her cruel father.
Philip needed a mother for his son, a mistress for his plantation.
It was a marriage of convenience.
Then it happened. The love they had tried to deny suddenly became a
blissful reality. . . only to be challenged by life's hardships and brutal
misfortunes.
